LIBRARY OF JAPANESE LITERATURE

THIS OUTCAST GENERATION

LUMINOUS MOSS

TAIJUN TAKEDA

THIS OUTCAST
GENERATION

LUMINOUS MOSS

translated by Yusaburo Shibuya and Sanford Goldstein

Representatives

For Continental Europe:
BOXERBOOKS, INC., *Zurich*
For the British Isles:
PRENTICE-HALL INTERNATIONAL, INC., *London*
For Australasia:
PAUL FLESCH & CO., PTY. LTD., *Melbourne*
For Canada:
m.g. hurtig ltd., *Edmonton*

Published by the Charles E. Tuttle Company, Inc.
of Rutland, Vermont & Tokyo, Japan

Copyright in Japan, 1967
by Charles E. Tuttle Co., Inc.

All rights reserved

Library of Congress Catalog No. 67–20951

First printing 1967

PRINTED IN JAPAN

TABLE OF CONTENTS

INTRODUCTION

WHEN JAPAN was defeated in 1945, Taijun Takeda was still a comparatively unknown writer living in Shanghai. The thirty-three-year-old Takeda saw how Shanghai Japanese, proud and triumphant for almost a decade, were tumbled overnight into a world of fear, humiliation, and panic. In their desperation to survive in the postwar chaos, even at the barest level of existence, they abandoned whatever they believed had made them uniquely Japanese. Like the narrator in *This Outcast Generation*,* they were surprised to discover how easy it was to put up with "loss of face," to "live shame down," though the process, like any therapeutic treatment, was slow and painful. There was no better place than Shanghai to give a Japanese the full realization of what it was like to be put to shame after the defeat of the homeland. With Taijun Takeda, however, the shock of recognition was particularly deep.

Yet his country's defeat should not have taken Takeda by surprise, much less bewilderment. As a student of Chinese literature he was much too familiar with the long history of China, with the idea of destruction through decline and fall of her states and leaders. In fact, Takeda's first major book, published only two years before the surrender, was a lengthy critical essay on the famous Chinese

---

* *Mamushi no Sue*, the Japanese title of Takeda's story, translates as *Generation of Vipers*. See Matthew 23:33 : *"Ye serpents, ye generation of vipers, how can ye escape the damnation of hell?"* A new title has been chosen for this translation in order to avoid confusion with Philip Wylie's book.

蝮のすえ・ひかりごけ

classic *Shi Chi (Historical Memories)* by Ssu-ma Chien (145–86 B.C.), castrated for displeasing his emperor in defending a personal friend, an army general who had surrendered to the Huns. Ssu-ma Chien had endured more than twenty years of disgrace and solitude in order to "review the world in [his] own terms." Takeda presented a detailed account of this 130-volume history of destruction and change, his eye always focused on the unique life of the chronicler. From the vast and confusing world of *Shi Chi* which recorded the conflicts and passions and destinies of individuals and states, Takeda summarized Ssu-ma Chien's world view with axiomatic assurance: all nations are doomed, though the doom itself allows mankind to survive.

As philosophy it was sufficiently pessimistic, but was there not some consolation in Takeda's discovery of a kind of "preordained harmony" in this cycle of destruction? When Japan surrendered, Takeda ought to have once more acknowledged this view of man and history and to have prepared himself for whatever lay ahead. But like the rest of his countrymen, he was totally dazed. At the moment of Japan's defeat he was to realize he was not as free or independent as he had led himself to believe. In spite of a vague though deep-rooted expectation that some day he would be able to separate himself from the militarism which had dominated Japan for so long, a militarism he loathed, he had actually been protected by his country's armies. Possibly this contradiction was typical of a youth brought up in a well-to-do family.

Born in Tokyo in 1912, Takeda was the second son in a temple family of high rank. He was raised as happily as any middle-class youngster. Of his parents he preferred his father, a man of simple tastes from the country, yet a scholar who taught Buddhistic philosophy. In middle school Takeda perhaps thought of himself as a future academician or scientist and showed no inclination for creative writing. The newspaper account of the suicide of the famous novelist Ryunosuke Akutagawa in 1927 made Takeda wonder why the death of a mere writer had caused such a sensation. Takeda's interest in Chinese literature after he entered high school in 1928 was merely part of one's training, but so intensely did he devote himself to reading classical and contemporary Chinese literature in books he suddenly discovered in the school library that he seldom attended classes. His joining an anti-imperialist leftist group, an activity typical of students at that time, further separated him from his formal studies.

Nevertheless, Takeda entered Tokyo University in 1931, where he was to major in Chinese literature, but in his first year he was arrested for distributing propaganda leaflets for his organization and was kept in confinement one month. When his father asked him to abandon this leftist movement, Takeda's acquiescence was typical of his obedience as a son. But the next year he also abandoned the university, having attended only a few lectures since matriculation. He had no need to worry about a livelihood: he was to succeed his father as temple priest. Yet the priesthood was not to his liking, especially at this time of religious decline. There was also the added stigma of living off contributions from others. Still, the obedient son proceeded to train for the priesthood and became a qualified *bonze*. Meanwhile, Takeda continued his study of Chinese language and literature, also participating in a circle of scholars with an anti-government bias as they devoted themselves to various studies on China. Among Takeda's friends were many Chinese students, and it was his association with a Chinese woman writer suspected of subversion that again led to his arrest and a month and a half confinement.

In October, 1937, Takeda was called to military duty and sent immediately to the battlefield of China. His experiences again caused him to think seriously about Ssu-ma Chien. Discharged from the army after two years, Takeda returned home, his first task being the subject of his long essay on *Shi Chi,* at the same time translating Chinese novels and trying his hand at original stories. After publishing *Ssu-ma Chien* in 1943, called *The World of Shi Chi* in later editions, he went the following year to Shanghai to work for the Japan-Chinese Cultural Association. It was in 1945 that he saw at first-hand what he had regarded as the inevitable fall of his own arrogant people, not that he considered himself freed from responsibility.

In the opening chapter of *Ssu-ma Chien,* Takeda had written: "Ssu-ma Chien was a man who remained alive in shame. Whereas any man of high rank would not have cared to survive, this man did. . . Completely driven to bay, fully aware of the base and disgusting impression he gave others, he brazenly went about the task of living. Even after his castration . . . Ssu-ma Chien continued to live, feeding and sleeping on a grief that day and night penetrated his entire body. He tenaciously persisted in writing *Shi Chi,* writing it to erase his shame, but the more he wrote, the more shame he felt." Takeda sounded elated in the discovery that a man so despised could evolve a philosophy which could turn the tables on the world that had so ruthlessly rejected him. But Takeda's voice was decidedly the voice of one who shared the same indignation, almost the identical shame of the castrated historian. For Takeda's own feelings to finally burst their bounds, he had to be a soldier in China, gun in hand as he stared at the mutilated bodies of Chinese peasants, their houses burned to ashes, their villages and towns destroyed.

Though Takeda had never been violently anti-imperialistic, he had nevertheless been part of the movement against Japanese imperialism in China, had loved the

Chinese, had majored in their literature and formed lasting friendships among them. As the son of a Buddhist priest and as a priest himself, he was supposed to preach the absolute negation of violence and killing. The realization of these multiple betrayals must have been torturing him as he witnessed what his countrymen had done to the Chinese. So intense was his guilt that one can imagine how relieved he must have felt in identifying himself with Ssu-ma Chien. But Ssu-ma Chien's feelings were based on righteous indignation, while all Takeda could do was kick himself, and identification was easier than downright self-accusation. Perhaps the objectivity which resulted in Takeda's masterful unity in *Ssu-ma Chien* was due partly to whatever confidence was left him that separated him from the ancient Chinese chronicler— some small, secret zone of safety which kept Takeda from being as "bad" as the castrated man. One more final blow was needed to hurl Takeda outside this zone of safety where he could dissect his very soul and ask himself what he was, what man was. That final blow was Japan's unconditional surrender. The novelist Takeda confronted it in its fullest impact, in all its immediacy. It is not surprising that *Shi Chi* and "The Revelation of St. John" were the two books he read for support during his dangerous day-to-day life in postwar Shanghai.

Takeda returned to Japan in 1946. The following year Hokkaido National University offered him a position as associate professor of Chinese Literature. At the same time his energetic career as novelist, critic, and essayist was underway. He published "Trial" (1947), a short story in which a young Japanese soldier, an intellectual, kills an old Chinese couple, not in the line of duty but out of pure whim as if to test a mathematical formula. During this year of hunting for war criminals and extracting confessions for war crimes and, by extension,

蝮のすえ・ひかりごけ

11

developing a hatred for war itself or the kind of social system that engenders war, Takeda's exposure of the dangerous potentiality in all of us to become senseless murderers was poignantly shocking. *This Outcast Generation* (1947), his first full-length story, which he saturated with his Shanghai experiences, placed him among the important postwar writers.

In 1948, he left teaching to devote his full energies to writing. Month after month he published stories and essays. In a time of hunger and black marketeering, Takeda seemed most alive, most sensitive, most hard-working. His glaringly colorful descriptions of human beings driven to bay under extremity perfectly corresponded to the postwar era, the Japanese nation's precarious survival in a world where the old values had apparently gone bankrupt. In one story after another Takeda posed radical questions that forced his readers to confront the meaning of human existence, whether he recorded his own experiences as a soldier in China or as a civilian in Shanghai or his bitter-funny apprenticeship as a Buddhist priest. The number of stories, novels, and essays he has written is astounding. Two decades after the war Takeda remains one of the most prolific writers in Japan. His materials, no longer limited to the autobiographical, represent bold forays into every area of human experience. "No phenomenon," said Takeda in a preface to a collection of his works, "escapes a novelist as uninteresting." As Japan has settled in the ways of peace, he has often been criticized for having an excessive interest in the dark side of human nature, but Takeda has retorted that in peace or war man is always faced with extremes, the chief of which is man himself. The mysterious complexity of man is Takeda's continual concern, especially so in *This Outcast Generation* and *Luminous Moss*.

This Outcast Generation is important not only because it

is the starting point in Takeda's career as a novelist, but because it provides a key to his unique thought, presented in this story in easily recognizable novelistic form. It offers a sharp contrast to the formal "disarray" of *Luminous Moss,* whose theme, on the other hand, parallels and intensifies the serious considerations of the earlier story.

Against the background of defeated Japanese in Shanghai, *This Outcast Generation* deals with the conflict of three Japanese men over the love of a Japanese woman. Compared to the gigantic military conflict that had just ended, the winning or losing of a woman seems almost petty, almost unworthy of comparison. Yet a parallel exists. War and love are intensely, peculiarly human affairs. The crucial point of the story is that human nature, submerged in the enormous mechanism of war, is re-examined in terms of individual human beings in their most private selves, in their most immediately felt experiences.

Without the impact of defeat, the narrator Sugi would never have been capable of murdering someone for love or for any other reason. In Sugi's attitude toward the woman's dying husband and the "powerful" man Karajima, we see what Sugi has learned by living in a place where, however unwillingly, he has been on the side of the strong. At the end of the war what has been brought home to him is not simply the grief or apathy of the defeated. What he realizes so starkly is the way war solved the conflict in such clear-cut, simple terms, so much so that it allowed no room for moral ambiguities. The victors in the war needed no justification or rationalization. Even the defeated felt willing to submit to the force of the "logic" of defeat. The narrator believes that justice of some supreme order has emerged. Perhaps such self-justification is part of the defense-mechanism of the subdued. Yet it is as if Sugi thinks himself freed from responsibility in life, as if some universal collapse, like apocalypse, has come true. But most of all his view

蝮のすえ・ひかりごけ

13

borders on a naturalistic view of nature, applied in this situation to war and defeat. Sugi sincerely feels he may as well be killed. He has concluded that not many men do not deserve death. This sort of detachment or nihilism helps him to confront without compunction or guilt the dying husband, the man whose wife Sugi loves. The dying is part of the order of things and has nothing to do with what Sugi does or does not do with the man's wife. That the living are stronger than the dying is so obvious no justification whatever is needed.

The narrator is fully aware of the same reasoning in confronting Karajima, the man of power. While pursuing him, Sugi feels he is pursuing someone only to be killed. Sugi is prepared to say his own dying is also in the order of things. By a curious turn of events, however, the narrator becomes the victor. He ought to be overjoyed, yet finds himself totally despondent. Something he sees in the expression of the dying Karajima shocks him into another recognition. Sugi has always thought Karajima power incarnate, not a man, not a human being. At Karajima's death the narrator realizes for the first time that Karajima was also human, also mortal. What Sugi feels is not relief but something like compassion, an awareness of his solidarity with Karajima as human beings. The narrator's beliefs are jolted.

But already the very fact of Sugi's having gone out to "kill" in order to "protect" a woman has belied that belief. The dramatic moment of conversion occurs when Sugi becomes conscious that he is refusing to be a nonentity in the order of things, the logical force of which he had once accepted as if it were some divine decree. Once shaken in this belief, he finally becomes aware that his acquiescence to the order of things, that is, to his being a nonentity, is *actually* the reverse side of his unconscious desire to be the strong. He had suspected that to live was to survive but at the expense of other lives.

Now, with the death of Karajima and the imminent death of the husband, Sugi comes to learn the meaning of being the strong, the survivor, or as he expresses it aboard ship, the meaning of everything that concerns being alive. As he has survived Karajima and the sick man, being alive is assuredly surviving, but the realization of the absurdity, as the sick husband says, of some staying alive while others are dying overwhelms the narrator and initiates him into a further recognition that the living owe the dying the fact of living, that the strong are strong because of the weak. This recognition of the link between survivor and survived may be called compassion or responsibility.

Thus *This Outcast Generation* considers man as a tension between individuals and history and as a contradiction in that tension. The theme is a far cry from the survival of the fittest; it is rather a hymn to humanitarianism, to the links in the great chain of existence.

But if to stay alive is to survive even if one has to murder, it requires only a further step for Takeda to insist that the survivor must, at the same time, be prepared to be survived or even to be murdered to help others to survive. *Luminous Moss* (*Hikarigoke*, 1954) is the dramatic presentation of this further step.

Before being confronted with the most unusual of unusual events, the reader is introduced to scenes of quite ordinary human lives in a calm natural environment. These scenes may serve as effective contrast; but, more important, they reveal Takeda's conviction that human existence itself, however serene in appearance, contains a mysterious tension, a horrifying contradiction. In Takeda's apparently leisurely and relaxed travelogue style, the reader can notice many suggestions of conflict, movements against life to perpetuate life. In fact, Takeda's first reference to cannibalism is made immediately after the narrator has observed the humblest of plants, the

蝮のすえ・ひかりごけ

15

luminous moss, which survives so precariously inside the cave. The implications behind the episode of cannibalism and the life of the plant are instantly fused in the narrator's mind: ". . . I was so fascinated by this 'incident of eating human flesh' that I could almost feel the 'creases of my mind' contract with a snap. . . I was conscious that the subject was turning from second to second into small black pellets in the depths of the 'Makkaushi Cave' of my mind, beginning to function furiously and to rave, urging and imploring for the earliest possible release." This peculiar mode of identification is based on a fundamental attitude that regards every living thing, human or plant, as equal in the continuation of life itself. The outlook is obviously religious, ascribable to the underlying spirit of Buddhism to which Takeda is so closely related by family and race.

The Captain, who has committed the gravest of sins, does not offer any legal or religious argument of self-justification. He does not try, through retaliation, to degrade the whole of humanity by marking it with the Sign of the Beast. He does not flaunt the courtroom spectators with the truth, a truth so horrible that mankind has been careful to avoid confronting it: that all life feeds upon itself to keep itself going. The Captain simply acknowledges the factual character of human existence, its tension and contradiction, under which he has learned to endure. Eventually the reader is forced to feel the full weight of the Captain's repetition of "bearing up." And the very acknowledgment of this "bearing up" points to Takeda's faith in man's peculiar capacity for transcendence in spite of the earth we are so mired in.

The profound questions raised by Takeda are difficult to present and answer in the conventional structure of the novel. Thus Takeda has sometimes been criticized for his narrative techniques. Yet the essay-in-story that is peculiarly Takeda's is pungently provocative. Takeda's existential-Buddhistic identity-of-all reveals him as a writer at once religious while equally committed to the brutality and illogicality of life itself. *This Outcast Generation* and *Luminous Moss* place Takeda at the very center of a compassionate view of troubled man and foreshadow the creation of the first serious religious novel in postwar Japanese literature, a task Takeda has recently indicated he wishes to make his lifework.

Yusaburo Shibuya
Meiji University, Tokyo

Sanford Goldstein
Purdue University, West Lafayette, Indiana

蝮のすえ・ひかりごけ

THIS OUTCAST GENERATION

I

—PERHAPS it's easier to go on living than you think.

I had laid my pillow on the concrete platform used for drying laundry, and I was relaxing in the sun. I took a sunbath there every morning after coming out of my dim back room. In the corner, as usual, were two chickens pecking away at leftover rice and withered vegetables. From the alley below came the almost threatening voices of Chinese haggling over bargains from the Japanese. The voices of the Japanese were low, feeble, and confused, so their customers sounded even more overbearing in their abuse. Only the voices of Japanese children at play were full of energy and happiness. Oddly enough, those joyful cries made the parents even more irritable.

—Since everyone's apparently able to get along like this.

With my weak vision it looked to me as if the wall of a theatre beyond the house roofs stood out garishly white. It seemed to float radiantly white out of the blue winter sky.

—You can lose a war, see your country collapse. And still you can go on living.

Before I had realized it, the shop windows of even the Japanese were decorated with flags of Nationalist China and photographs of Chiang Kai-shek and his wife. I too had bought a small photograph from an old man peddling pictures of the couple. The snapshot had sold like hotcakes.

—All you need is a guardian angel.

To prepare for the inspection tours of the Chinese police, I had put the photograph between the pages of a

蝮
の
す
え

notebook. When the Chinese national anthem was sung at the movies, the audience stood up and so did I, my eyes obediently on the flag and a framed picture of Sun Yat-sen. I had stood up apathetically, like a puppet, and then sat down, and the movie over, I had gone out through the crowds of Chinese teenagers pushing me around. I had merely listened indifferently as the agitated audience cried out simultaneously over a violently anti-Japanese film. Sometimes I had no expression on my face, sometimes I smiled reluctantly. Whatever the occasion, the only thing I really marveled at was my own ability to somehow continue living when I so easily might have been dead. At first, I believed that bearing the humiliation kept me going. But when I thought over the defeat and its aftermath, I felt no shame, nothing in fact. My blank face and reluctant smile were merely the mask by which I was simply living without any humiliation whatsoever.

I started to earn my keep by writing out documents in Chinese. There was no end of callers. Since my landlord was a broker, his customers of the past fifteen years came to me in a constant stream. They were so totally confused that they even talked respectfully to me! Even in defeat life marches on. As if to confirm this principle, clients came to me to lodge complaints of various kinds. A pale old man once asked me to help him after his employer had been robbed and kidnapped. Unless the police were notified immediately, his boss would be in for some real trouble. So urged, I had gone into my dark back room on the second floor. Even in broad daylight I turned on the electricity. I spread out my carbons on a tangerine crate. I sluggishly went about my task with the help of a Japanese-Chinese dictionary. And the job finished, I was paid off. I would hesitate in giving my fee. The currency of the puppet-government was still in circulation, and I had to figure out the price of four packs of cigarettes. The money I earned came out of human misery. Beautiful reflection that! It's a pity the thought lasted only two or three days after I had gone into my trade. I wanted my sake and rich food so that trouble and customers were an absolute prerequisite.

Someone would be evicted tomorrow. In one way or another, someone would have to move his belongings into the Japanese compound. A Japanese man desired Chinese citizenship in order to return to his family in Taiwan. A Japanese drafted to dive for salvage wanted to give written notice of illness—that was how eager he was to get home. Some Japanese wished to illegally convert the goods they had on hand into money, others to open street stalls. A Korean-born reporter came. A blind person came. A pregnant woman came. A Japanese merchant who promised to pay me anything I asked and a sick man hardly able to walk because of malnutrition, they came too. I undertook anything. I prepared documents audaciously. I wrote irresponsibly. All I cared about was getting my documents approved. Sometimes I chose expressions designed to move the heartstrings of officials in charge of us Japanese living in China. Sometimes I developed watertight arguments. I wrote grandiloquently. I wrote half-truths that favored my clients. I finally reached the point of writing barefaced lies. At the very least, however, what I did write was understood. That was why most of my documents got through. My customers came to offer their thanks. Before I realized it, I was gaining their confidence. Not only was I a popular transcriber. I began to be looked upon as a reliable guy!

My only thought was to get paid. I never felt I was working for the benefit of Japanese residents. Those that depended on me in this way I pitied. I found the world ridiculous in which a person as irresponsible, as incompetent as I, could still be useful. The world was too flimsy, too dissatisfying. Formerly, before coming to

蝮
の
す
え

Shanghai and even later, I had studied hard, worked hard, thought hard. At that time not a soul had trusted me. After the end of the war I didn't study, didn't work, didn't think. But in people's eyes I was changing into a man of integrity, at least to the extent that I had never before been considered for the role. No longer did I have any ideals, any faith. I was merely breathing, and that, apparently, was what people expected of me. I fell into the habit of looking sober as a judge. No matter what the proposition, I wasn't surprised. That was the kind of person my customers were seeking advice from about their personal affairs. A man married to a Chinese woman wanted to know if he ought to get a divorce or not. A Japanese wife about to run off to her sweetheart just before her repatriation told me her scheme. Occasionally, therefore, I reached the position of the Catholic priest who lends an ear to confessions and vows.

One morning I was drinking some sake left over from the night before. I gulped down a cup. Though the wine was beginning to sour a little, I was in a hurry to get drunk. Then I intended to write a poem I had called "The Man Shot to Death." The execution of a German war criminal I had seen in a newsreel had made quite an impression on me . . . Shots. Inside the white smoke the upper part of the bound body jerked forward. With that it was over. It had really been simple. As plain as day. So truthful as to be intensely satisfying. In it was something beyond logic. It had pleased me immensely.

> Upper torso in a forward fall—
> Why?
> Gravity's law.

As I was jotting down these expressions in bold strokes, my landlady called up to me that I had a visitor, a young lady who had come a few days before.

I put a padded robe over my wrinkled workclothes and went down. Young? Probably her, I said to myself, remembering one of my clients.

Her husband was an invalid, but the real estate company that owned their house had demanded they vacate in three days. There wasn't a thing she could do by herself, so she had asked me to write a petition to the authorities.

My visitors always waited inside the front door. The sunlight through the seven or eight sheets of glazed glass in the roof made the doorway brighter than my room. When I had first seen that woman in winter clothing standing in the pale light, a shudder had gone through me. What had impressed me was her tall, slim body, her white face, like some flower at evening, her attitude, shy in a lovely sort of way yet seductively coquettish. I had felt as if something I had forgotten over a long period of time had suddenly turned up, a fantasy I had once believed in when I hadn't lost my aim in life.

"I'll do it."

In an efficient businesslike way, I had learned the essentials from her and had gone upstairs and composed a beautiful piece of prose. I had handed her the document I was so proud of, and without smiling, I deliberately demanded twice my usual fee. My business was the writing of documents, and I had long ago become contemptuous of romantic sentimentality. I had given up any feelings of anxiety about matters not related to my trade.

"Is that enough?" she had said, taking some bills out of her patent leather bag and putting them down on the mats. "It's probably been very hard on you since you started doing this kind of work," she had said, her eyes large and friendly as she looked up at me standing there.

"I've often read your poems. My husband likes them too. He's always asking about you." It had seemed to me she was reminiscing.

"What's that?" I had said, embarrassed, as if the flow of blood in my body had suddenly reversed itself. Why, just as I was about to receive my fee, had she started talking about my earlier poems, those terrible sentimental pieces?

—Always asking about me, did she say? Listen to that!

"Take this to the Board and have them sign it," I had said roughly, gathering up the money.

She had thanked me, and when her beautiful legs were no longer in view beyond the dark door, I had tramped up the narrow staircase. I was so excited I felt dizzy. I had even bruised my right ankle as I missed a step.

Luckily I was drunk when she came again. After all, wasn't she a young wife, and even after the war, with plenty of money, was she really in need of anything?

"Well?" I asked rudely. "Did it get through?"

"Thanks to you, they made an immediate inquiry. We don't have to leave."

Her red and white checked sweater caused her white face to look even more dazzling. "Someone gave these to me," she said, holding out a pack of imported cigarettes. There was no sign she intended to return.

"Are you free now? I'd like to talk something over with you."

"Well? What is it?"

"It's difficult to talk here."

"In my room then?"

I took the cigarettes, worth several times my fee, and went upstairs. What a beautiful, graceful animal she seemed as she sat near me in my small dark room with its walls barren except for an electric light and a gas meter. Instantly my wretched back room was filled with scent and warmth, with something like the radiance of women. I spread out a dirty blanket and had her sit at the same time I did. Again I poured some wine into my cup from the half-gallon bottle.

"You men are lucky you're able to drink. You can forget everything."

I felt oppressed each time she moved her lovely legs in their silk stockings. I swore at myself, resisting, getting malicious even.

"We go on living, putting up with the humiliation. We're miserable. It's almost impossible to talk about."

"You don't say," I said with deliberate sarcasm.

"All we have is pain and humiliation." Suddenly her expression changed. She looked down, crying, her shoulders shaking. It annoyed me, yet I found her weeping charming enough. She was so gentle, so luscious, I couldn't help feeling sympathetic. Still, I wasn't going to let it get the better of me. She wasn't the only one that wanted to cry. If I could have, I might have tried a tear or two myself.

Yet her last remark, confirmed by her tears, had certainly turned out to be painful and humiliating for me too. I was drunk, but the pain I felt in her words refused to go away. I might reject them, ignore them, but I did feel their significance.

"I guess you know about Karajima. He was my husband's employer. What do you think of him, Mr. Sugi?"

Of course I knew how influential Karajima had been as a propagandist for the Japanese army. I had even seen him once, a handsome, well-built, fair-complected man. He was quite adept in his role as hero and gentleman. He wore tasteful ties, the best of clothes. In spite of myself, I could still accept his absolute self-confidence in treating others as subhuman. But I detested the way he played the sophisticate that knows every thought and emotion of the man he's with. It was stupid and depressing to be governed by such men of power. I had listened to his ranting voice and polished speeches, and even after spitting, I had been left with an aftertaste of something dirty. But when the war ended, I had forgotten him. I had forgotten his nastiness too. Once you started talking about nastiness, everything, yourself included, seemed nasty.

Her husband had worked in Karajima's printing division and later had been sent to Hankow. She had to remain alone in Shanghai. Karajima had offered to find her a room, and on the day they were to inspect it, she had gone to Karajima's office. When he had closed the door after her, he told her he had liked her from the first and violently threw his arms around her.

"Some of his workers ought to have been in the next room. I struggled and cried out, but no one came."

Though she might have been upset, she easily told me everything. Sometimes she stole a glance at me with those beautiful eyes of hers. Apparently she wanted to see if I was disturbed. I didn't let on that I was.

"He was like an animal," she said. Her words and look seemed to point an accusing finger at all men. I began thinking that if I had the power, I too—I even imagined that I was the one, not Karajima, who had those arms around her. What it had amounted to, at any rate, was that she had let him have her. She had lived on without even a thought of suicide.

"He had me every night after that." I kept staring at her body, and that searing pain I so patiently endured was possibly not unpleasant.

Out went a Karajima directive to Hankow, so her husband was stationed there until the end of the war. For the duration she had been Karajima's possession. Try as she might to hide from him, up he drove in his car. All the neighbors and her husband's friends knew about it, but no one stopped Karajima. When her husband had finally returned to Shanghai, he was totally emaciated from a terrible case of diarrhea. He was bedridden from the moment they had carried him off the truck. She was still kept by Karajima. He was generous with money and supplies. And sometimes he summoned her from the bedside of her stricken husband.

Her husband knew about their relationship and kept abusing her with it. She admitted the affair and asked him to forgive her. He refused to take the medicine purchased with Karajima's money, but without these funds they wouldn't have been able to afford electricity, water, even the sheets the invalid was lying on. He was tormented by the thought that his friends had so contemptuously forsaken him. It was even more painful to have her consoling him. He often kept telling her how detestable she was, yet he said she deserved pity.

"He's good. And so like a child."

She rolled her tear-drenched handkerchief into a ball, and opening her compact, she began putting on some make-up. She colored her slightly opened lips a fresh red, and as she powdered her face, her cheeks kept expanding and contracting. She was skillful, thorough.

"Well, how about now? Karajima I mean."

"I've definitely left him. I'm determined to hate him until I die. He'll be caught soon since he's a war criminal."

A cold, blunt expression was on her face. When she finished speaking, I picked up my cup. I felt my grim smile had somehow distorted my face. I couldn't explain why I felt only suspicious then.

Did she really despise Karajima? Wasn't there more pleasure than misfortune in having given herself to him? Her resolutions to the contrary, she had, however half-heartedly, kept up the relationship so that some desire other than monetary might have been behind it. In her eagerness to live comfortably, or if not that at least adequately, I doubted if there was any self-accusation or humiliation behind the affair.

I imagined she had the same detestable human instinct to survive by merely living, by forgetting all about pain

蝮
の
す
え

29

and humiliation, especially when I was so well aware of that same instinct in me. The simple assault of her charm made me feel even more convinced of the truth of my observation. I felt sick, depressed.

"I believe in you. That's why I've gone into all of this."

She poured me some wine.

"But I really came on my husband's orders. He doesn't want to see any of his former friends. He's read your poems and believes in you. He wants to talk to you. Can you come just once as a favor to him? He'll be overjoyed. We're so miserable all the time! How about tomorrow? It's best to come early. The past few days he's been quite ill."

She had returned after making me promise to visit the next day. At the same time I was worrying about the dust blowing all over the concrete platform I was lying on, the particles sticking to my skin, which hadn't been exposed to a bath for a month, I kept wondering if I ought to go. It made little difference if I did or not. Of course, there was plenty to interest me. Yet whether I went or not didn't really matter. There wasn't a soul to accuse me of not doing something to help them out of their situation.

As I walked along, a youngster selling candy kept pestering me. I find these kids annoying except when I'm drunk. At a street corner I saw a Japanese having his hat stolen by a young delinquent. That troubled, weak-looking face should have evoked some sympathy in me, but all the same I couldn't help finding it disagreeable. He had run a few steps after the thief and had stopped, relinquishing his hat, stealing a glance at me. I couldn't help feeling disgusted by the sight of his helpless eyes.

I reached the woman's apartment, the Indian gate-keeper opening the iron gate for me. He looked sharply at my Japanese-resident armband. I rang the doorbell three doors beyond.

She seemed quite delighted as she ran down the stairs. It made me feel good to have caused that happiness in her. But I sensed the contradiction. She was too lively, quite out of keeping with the daily depression she had talked about.

As I took off my shoes at the threshold of the third floor apartment, I saw the signs of a sick person in the next room. He must have been lying in bed waiting for me. I felt the tension with which he must have waited. Perhaps it was a momentous interview for him. To me it shouldn't have meant a thing. I would have been disgusted with myself had I made it momentous when it was nothing of the sort.

She offered me a cushion to sit on, a colorful one.

The invalid was so very thin that the flatness of his covers made it seem as if his body wasn't under them. At first he turned sideways to look at me, but he glanced back up at the ceiling right away. At that very moment heavy wrinkles, like a monkey's or a baby's just after its birth, formed on his face. He was crying. It was embarrassing to see his neck and shoulders shaking as he tried to stop himself. His forehead and cheeks were an ugly red.

The tears made it difficult for him to speak. His voice often grew weak, gave out.

"At first he had only diarrhea, but then a bad case of pleurisy set in. The fluid's been accumulating, so his heart is slightly out of place."

Her own voice was clear and crisp as she handed her husband a handkerchief and forced him to take some water. I was surprised by the speed and energy of each of her actions. How conspicuously youthful the color of her arms, the roundness of her calves!

"I have no friends to confide in, so I thought . . . you

蝮
の
す
ゑ

31

. . . you would do me the favor of listening. It's . . . such a humiliating story . . . So humiliating I can't tell it to just anyone."

I forced myself to look at his face, which was too weak and dried up to convey the violence of his emotions. It wasn't a pretty sight, yet I was reminded of my own good health. It caused me to feel self-confident, even superior.

"I'm no saint. And I'm not a person you tell secrets to. But I thought I'd better come up to see you. It was rude of me just to drop in," I said.

"I . . . I don't expect you to do . . . anything in particular for me. I just wanted to talk to someone like you. It's unbearable to be lonely," he said.

He looked much younger than me. He had been good-looking. Those clear, nervous, agitated eyes seemed to be anticipating my thoughts way ahead of time. The slightest change in my face caused a shadow of fright to skirt across his eyes. For a fraction of a second a bright trace of insanity was glittering in that shadow.

"Lately my wife keeps saying she wants to die. Not me. I've . . . things I want to do."

"You have? I envy you. There's not a single thing I care to do."

"You're wrong. You don't realize . . . you're doing something already. I will too. I'll do . . . what I couldn't do during the war. I must do it! I've been totally useless . . . up to now. This time at least . . . I'll do what I want! I'll get strong! I'll do something . . . to destroy men like Karajima! If I can't . . . then I'm going to be a thousand times more evil than he is!"

The feverish and excited invalid had been overexerting himself by speaking. I knew he'd die soon. It was strongly foreshadowed by his yellow skin, by the bridge of his thin nose. It was obvious he'd never achieve any of his goals. I felt no pity, only oppression.

"I've no contact with anyone . . . any longer. They

all . . . hate me. She's cheated on me, and . . . I'm living off the money she gets from him. It's not right . . . to let this pass! It's terrible . . . to be buried with such shame. Without wiping out even a small portion of it!"

Her husband's remarks about her made her glance at me, her beautiful eyebrows shaped into a frown.

"It's terrible . . . to be hated," he said, stopping momentarily to regulate his breathing. Then he recounted the dream he had the night before.

He had become a leper. The offensive odor given off by his mouth and body made him unbearable to his wife. Seeing her frightened face fill with hatred, he felt he was losing his mind. She ran away and he pursued her, catching her, holding her tight, that terrible odor coming out of his mouth and from his body so that he had finally become aware of his own stench. She spat at him, cursing him, then fled. His loneliness had made him cry out.

"When I woke up and found I'd only been dreaming, I felt I was lucky not to have leprosy. I really felt relieved my sickness was just ordinary."

"That's all you dream about, isn't it?" she said.

She looked tense as she prepared our tea. She was trying to smile but couldn't.

"My dream's about Karajima. I murder him in my dream."

She spoke casually, but her words sounded theatrical, melodramatic. They had the false ring of something feminine. Her husband's eyes became even more dismal.

"Mr. Sugi!" he suddenly cried out in a high thin voice. "I can't believe her! While Karajima's alive, I can't believe anything she says!"

Again he began crying. This time he didn't try to stifle it, crying openly, strange sounds in his throat mixed in with his words.

"You shouldn't talk like that in front of Mr. Sugi! It's too cruel! It's too much!"

"You keep on lying, that's why!"

"No matter what I say, you take it as a lie! I can't go on living like that!"

"You're living, aren't you? Aren't you living without a care in the world?"

His crying, staccato-like voice was a sick man's. But her tearful voice, even as she tried to suppress it, was bursting with the vigor of youth. Those two sobbing voices continued, sometimes intermingling, sometimes separating.

I took out one of the imported cigarettes I had received the day before. I had no matches, and she quickly pulled out a box of foreign-make from her pocket. She smiled, embarrassed by the tears on her cheeks.

"Oh, your tea's cold! Well, I'll serve you a nice lunch!"

I begged off since I wasn't feeling well. "It's my stomach."

"You're not going home!"

Her husband stopped crying, his expression changed, I imagined, since he thought I was about to leave at that moment. The look of sadness in his eyes seemed to indicate he didn't know what to do. It was as if I had suddenly struck him.

"I guess it's unpleasant to see something like this. But please stay. Just a little longer. We've no one to rely on. You're the only one we can trust."

"Oh, it hasn't been that unpleasant. It's just that I—" I wanted to say I couldn't stand being trusted. But I stopped for that would have sounded phony. In a situation of this sort, no matter how seriously I might have used such words, they would have been superficial. I had long stopped being in dead earnest about anything.

The couple recovered their composure and reverted to small talk. I sat ten more minutes before standing up.

"Can I join you for lunch next time? Frankly, the oysters I ate last night didn't agree with me."

The invalid was resigned, yet satisfied. A gentle expression was on his face.

"Please come again. I'll be waiting."

"I will. I'm glad I came. I like you both, more than I thought I would. I've really felt close to you."

That was true. I had sensed that they had been ashamed of themselves, that they were grappling, however hopelessly, with life in all seriousness. They had suffered between themselves long enough. After my words I saw a genuine look of pleasure light up the man's eyes. It wasn't an exaggeration to call it that. For quite a while I hadn't seen anything that simple and straightforward. He automatically offered me his thin hand, but he pulled it back fearfully.

She came with me when I was going downstairs. As she went alongside me, she was almost touching me.

"I was delighted you came today," she said, turning at once to face me before opening the downstairs door.

It seemed odd to hear her say, "Don't desert us, please. If you do, we won't forgive you! My husband will hold a grudge against you, and so will I!" Her words didn't sound that flippant, for apparently she had really given some thought to not being taken lightly. In fact, I found her words strangely profound.

"Don't be disgusted with me. Please protect me. Lend me some of your strength, and I'll come back to life again." She suddenly lowered her voice. "He may even die tomorrow. Understand?" Her eyelids narrowed over her eyes, which, ablaze with fever, were riveted on me.

As I went out the iron gate, firecrackers were going off everywhere, ringing in my ears. The next day would be the old calendar New Year. Red streamers were posted on the pillars and doors of every house. Some of the streamers had already been torn to shreds and were fluttering in the dust along the streets. Those fluttering scraps looked strangely vivid among the withered leaves and trash. A mother with her baby bundled up in a red cloth rode by on a rickshaw. Somehow those red colors seemed warm, mystical. As I walked back, I saw only the vivid reds of the festival. Men and women sat or walked or gathered in groups, their hands and faces dirty, their blue clothing worn out, filthy. Those men and women were trying to greet the New Year in some small way. For the first time apparently, I discovered that all these Chinese were living together, indifferent to me and other Japanese.

When I knocked at the back door, my landlady opened it. She smiled and then brought out a bottle of sake for me. If was a gift from the Japanese Self-Governing Council.

"You can celebrate the New Year," she said.

I took the bottle and went up to my room. The sake was sweet and thick. That night I had to finish a detailed report on a confiscated Japanese factory. I had to write in English or Chinese the name, serial number, and value of at least two hundred different kinds of precision machines. A catalogue and dictionary were on my crate. I made up my mind to buy some navel oranges with part of my fee. I would bring them as a gift when I visited the invalid.

By evening I was half-finished. I was drunk and tired. I felt a pain in my side, and my fingers could hardly move. My eyes kept getting weaker. Some men came into the alley to sell bread. A few came with pastry. All of them were Japanese reduced to becoming peddlers. No one bought anything from them.

Aoki dropped in. He wrote editorials for a Japanese newspaper.

"Why haven't you been to the Art Association meetings?"

"I haven't felt like it."

"The day after tomorrow the Cultural Division of the

Chinese Control Office is calling everyone together. How about coming with me?"

"Can't. I've got documents to do."

I couldn't help feeling how superficial the word "culture" was. Aoki kept on talking about the Chinese People's Court and other topics. They didn't interest me either. All I could think about were those yellow oranges I had seen, lustreless, piled high.

When Aoki left, I crawled into bed and tried to doze off. It was windy out, and someone kept knocking at the back door. I had a hunch it was for me. It was annoying to be plagued with callers. I heard a woman's voice. The thought rushing through me that she had come drove away my heavy, uncomfortable drowsiness. I sat up in bed. She was coming, coming! I was drunk. There was no telling how callous or even violent I would become.

She opened the door, and I heard her brown raincoat rustling, her outer clothing visible through it. Small drops of water sparkled minutely on her coat. "Just a second!" she said. She stepped over my bedding on the mats, unfastened the window, and quietly opened it. The dark grating was drenched with rain. "It's all right. He didn't follow me." She closed the window after peering down into the alley. "I bumped into Karajima on the street. I told him I was going to your place, and he said he'd come with me. I broke away from him and ran here."

Her wet cheeks were pale. She looked tired.

"Is he still hanging around?"

"Yes. I even met him the last time I was here."

Her face was quite strained.

"He can't forget me. He said so himself. Strange, isn't it? —I brought you a snack. Have it with your sake."

"You came out just for that?"

"Yes. I really wanted you to have it." She took some teabiscuits from a black box. They were fried brown and looked homemade.

"Tomorrow's the New Year. I wonder if I can come see you?" she said.

I hadn't mentioned her sick husband, nor had she made the slightest reference to him.

"Quite free and easy, am I not?"

"Yes, free and easy."

"Perhaps I'm slightly insane."

"A little," I said.

But I had my mind on Karajima. I wanted a detailed account of him. In spite of her reluctance *he* was what fascinated me.

"He's really all steamed up about you after all."

"It looks that way." She showed her annoyance at my having mentioned it. "That conceited thing went so far as to ask *me* to save him! I was dumbfounded. It's too late for jokes like that. With the war crimes he's going to be charged with, he's really losing his mind."

"You mean he asked *you* to help him?"

"Odd, isn't it? A man asking a woman to help him out!"

That surprised me too. My only impression of Karajima was as the man of power you can't help despising. I had thought of him as an annoying insect, not as a man with feelings similar to my own. I didn't really loathe him— that is, I didn't really think about him. So I wasn't quite ready to accept her words at face value.

"It's not even a question of saving him. Since it's absolutely impossible for me to. Even if I could, I don't want to be dragged into the mess he's in. I definitely left him, you know, when the war ended."

She sounded phony to me. That was what she had said at our last meeting. I suspected her words were false, but she probably hoped they didn't sound that way.

"It strikes me he's not the type to scream for help. It's just that he needs you."

"I don't know about that. At any rate, I'm afraid.

While he's alive, I can't sleep." She gave me the same look she had used at the door of her apartment. "Will you protect me? Will you love me? I love you."

"You mean—?" I might have felt overjoyed, but even then I wanted to equivocate. It was all so new. In contrast to me, she looked absolutely certain.

"I'm really in a difficult situation. You see that, don't you? So I'm quite serious. Don't lie. If you love me, say so. A half-hearted reply won't settle anything. I'm honestly in love with you."

"I love you. Of course I do. But maybe I can't protect you. I can't protect anyone."

"You love me then?"

"Yes."

"That's enough for me. That's fine. If *only* you do. Well, perhaps it's difficult for you to protect me." There was no malice in her smile. "You do seem lazy."

"I haven't had any experience along that line."

She grabbed my shoulders and stood up and kissed me. Her lips were quite soft. When she was about to move away, I put my arms around her and gave her a fairly hard kiss.

I felt she had planned this scene. I was certain she was following a script. But that didn't upset me. I didn't even feel I was being taken in. In fact, the thought that she was precious to me kept steadily increasing.

"But can you love me? Can you love a woman Karajima had?" Her eyes were riveted on me, her face oddly static, almost blank, because of her own passion.

"Love me! Think of me with pity! Oh, I want him killed! I wish someone would kill him now, right away!" Clinging to me and drawing her face close and sobbing quietly, she blurted out her threat. Apparently she couldn't control her feelings. All the while I continued holding her against me, I clearly recalled Karajima's face. He was no longer unrelated to me. Through her I

蝮
の
す
え

39

was conscious of his body. He came so surprisingly close I could actually smell his breath.

"Before you said Karajima acted like he was coming here, didn't you?"

"Yes." She seemed caught up in some dark thought. "That's been his intention for a long time, I think. I'm sure of it."

"Alone? Why?"

"Probably to talk something over with you."

"But I don't know him that well."

"I didn't know you either, did I? Isn't that true? He suspects I'm relying on you. He's quite desperate. We have no time to lose."

"Is it that bad?"

"Yes. You've never had your life hanging in the balance, have you?"

"Sure. But now it's different. Now I'm hanging only on the side of life. I'm not on a tightrope anymore."

"Sometimes a man risks his life even when he doesn't intend to. Can you kill Karajima?"

". . . Yes. But I don't want to."

"Don't you think he deserves it?"

"I guess so. There aren't many men who don't deserve killing."

She smiled faintly and seemed to be even more lost in thought. In spite of her eager and naive way of speaking, that look came from the intense and instinctive way she was living, feeling. It seemed to me we were both saturated with darkness and violence.

"What's this? A poem?" She picked up "The Man Shot to Death" and read what I had written. Already it no longer appealed to me. Today I had fallen, collapsed. When I compared myself at this moment with the poem itself, I found it was annoyingly smooth and superficial. I had to make it deeper.

"What do you think about every day?" A trace of roguery was in her gentle smile. "Even *you* do some thinking?"

"No," I said, reluctantly smiling.

"Will you come see me again?"

I recalled the bedridden invalid. I saw she did too. "I'll bring him some oranges."

"Good. I'll be waiting." She pressed my fingers firmly. "But don't force yourself to since I'll be coming here."

"I'll definitely come at least once more." I deliberately kept myself from walking her back. I had had enough uniqueness for one day. It was already more than enough.

II

A CHINESE sentinel rebuked me the day after New Year's. I was not only drunk. I was guilty. On the way to the Japanese Self-Governing Council is a post with a sentinel on duty. A regulation requires the Japanese to bow in front of him. I had often passed and bowed. If I was alone, it was an easy thing to do. But I was quite self-conscious when several men and women lowered their heads in rapid succession as they walked ahead of me or when I was talking to an acquaintance and happened to pass by. That was the moment I felt myself resisting. Many Chinese often came to a standstill and watched our performance. For the most part, the guards didn't give us any outlandish orders, didn't even shout at us.

That morning a well-built Japanese about thirty years old was walking ahead of me. Squaring his shoulders and apparently marching along steadily, he seemed charged with physical energy. He was wearing a business suit, but he looked like an ex-military man. His hat still on and with self-conscious dignity, he was about to go by the sentinel. Then the man violently cleared his throat, spat, and walked on. The short sentinel stopped just as he was

蝮

の

す

え

41

about to shout at the man. That was when I came along. I was hatless. Not a soul was around, but I didn't bow. The sentinel called me to a halt. I crossed the street and came over to him. "Why didn't you bow? Stand there," he said. The voice of that short, young sentinel wasn't even threatening. He even looked like a nice young man. Standing at attention, I said in Chinese, "I'm very sorry." My drunkenness made me sway. "All right, move along," he said suddenly, turning aside. I didn't feel particularly embarrassed. In fact, standing at attention in the morning in front of a sentinel on a street in a strange land and bowing and apologizing seemed to exactly fit my personality. I understood the feelings of that young man who hadn't taken off his hat and had walked past the guard while purposely clearing his throat so strenuously. But those feelings could no longer exist in me. I had certainly broken the regulations often enough, but not because I had wanted to. I had simply been careless or lazy. I felt it natural to be rebuked and punished for violating laws. But even if I were rebuked or punished, I had almost become indifferent to it. I had made up my mind that I would often be scolded.

Immediately after the war I had frequently broken through blockades the authorities had set up. The crossroads were watched by groups of ten or more soldiers and policemen. I would cut through those blockades on my bicycle. They would shout at me from all sides and rush to grab my bike. Pedaling for all I was worth, I would shout back at them. All of a sudden the thick rope stretched across the road would strike against my arms. A burning pain. The skin would be scraped off my arms. The rope would slip away from me. So near would a few of the guards come that they almost grabbed my bike. I'd ignore them and make my bike race on. At that moment it would dawn on them that I was one of those half-cocked drunks. Then they'd only pretend they were after me. I'd escape with the night winds rushing by, and I'd end up at the edge of the French Settlement.

Sometimes they caught me. There were places, for example Japanese elementary schools, which, before we knew it, had been confiscated in order to house Chinese soldiers on their arrival from Chungking. Once I pedaled along a dark gravel road and was suddenly warned to halt. A gun-toting soldier stood in the dark. I kept on going right past him. Unfortunately, gravel roads aren't for fast riding. A soldier grabbed my handlebars. Instantly my bike fell sideways, and I rolled over on the ground. He held me by the arms and led me inside a gate. A table was set up in front of a tent, and someone, an officer apparently, was sitting there. Only that spot was glaringly bright.

"Who are you?"

"A Japanese."

"Japanese?"

Then his voice became mild. "What have you been up to?"

"Drinking at a friend's."

"Why didn't you stop when you were told to? Weren't you given an order? If you had stopped, we wouldn't be blaming you."

"No, you wouldn't."

They let me go and I went out the gate, picked up my bike, and rode on. Pedaling off after something like that, I always failed to keep my bike steady since I couldn't handle it as I wished. Somewhere one of its parts would be twisted or unfastened. But already I would have forgotten the incident. All I cared about was staying on that bike I could hardly control.

Right after the war I still had that childlike quality of performing such exciting feats, of having fresh adventures. Now, nothing like that remained in me. Those episodes were foolish acts that came from doing what was

蝮
の
す
え

43

beyond my power. I had no physical stamina. I had no power by which to give blow for blow. I was only deluding myself in feeling I could do anything. Pretending to be strong is unnecessary when you know your pretense is useless. You can live even if you don't pretend you're strong. They'll pardon you if you apologize. Everything will work out all right if you just let the bowing stop being painful. And even if it is, everything will work out for you if you persuade yourself it's not painful. It's easier to live by obeying the regulations. At least it's essential to be thought of as someone who does. But when I'm drunk, I forget that injunction. I imitate the strong man. Then when I sober up, I'm contemptuous of my extravagant delusions. Still, I can't deny in my heart of hearts that I'm forever concealing a deep-seated desire to perform the actions of a superman. In some meaningful way living is related to strength. To live is to survive. In one form or another a man lives because of his strength. I had merely been existing in order to exist. But even in existing, I wondered if I hadn't been wanting, thirsting, for strength.

"Can you kill Karajima?"

". . . Yes. But I don't want to."

A number of times since that night I had asked myself if I could kill him. I imagined various ways of doing it. I didn't feel I had to kill him, but it was hardly to be expected that I couldn't put him out of the way. Without letting myself get too keyed up, I had been able to feel the hardness of his head and chest, the thickness of his flesh.

That morning after I had been rebuked and pardoned, I went on toward the Self-Governing Council, and while walking alone, I suddenly began wondering if someone as worthless as me could kill Karajima. I could actually feel my strength, comparing it to the physical power of the young sentinel, the well-built Japanese who had passed without removing his hat, and Karajima. I imagined the weight of flesh and bone, the warmth and sweat and blood, charging into me. I felt how much life force I had even down to the most delicate parts of my arms and legs. Only then did I suddenly realize I was actually alive.

I stopped off at a market, a dreary, white concrete building two-stories high. Usually the square thick pillars lined up on the first floor were hidden by mobs of lively customers, but now those columns were nakedly exposed. Many of the Chinese shops inside were closed. The entire street was just about cleared of morning mist. It looked dead out. After I bought some of the oranges I had previously seen, I went up to visit the invalid.

"I was too upset last time," he said.

He was in better spirits. His wife had gone out. I found an unfinished pattern of brown woolen yarn still spread out where she had been sitting the time before. I imagined she was meeting Karajima somewhere.

I untied my package, took out an orange, and cut it with the jackknife I kept in my pocket.

When the invalid bit into the slice I gave him, the juice trickled from his mouth to his chin. He was in bed, his face turned away to the side. The juice ran down onto the towel covering his ice-filled rubber pillow.

"Ever since you came to see me, I've felt better. I can probably sail on the hospital ship if I keep up at this rate."

"Sure you can. A ship's on its way."

I knew about these ships since I had been asked to write letters for embarkation.

"They said we'd be among the first to be sent back." That meant his wife would go as his attendant. It was natural she should, but somehow I couldn't picture her going with him.

"Haven't you any intention of returning yet, Mr. Sugi?"

蝮
の
す
ゑ

45

"No. What would be the use even if I did? They say there's nothing to eat or drink in Japan."

"I live in the country. I don't expect to run short of anything. Stay with us for six months if you wish."

"Well, it's generous of you."

"Was your house destroyed?"

"Last March."

"What about your family?" he asked.

"There were two others, but they're dead. No one's left now."

My mother and younger sister were dead. After I got all mixed up during the war and even later, I couldn't remember what they looked like when I had met them the day before I had left for Shanghai. I had forgotten everything, the clothes they wore, what we talked about, whether we cried or laughed on saying good-bye. But when the invalid's frail voice had referred to my family, I suddenly felt I needed them. I was jolted, though only for a fraction of a second. I had no particular envy of the safe, peaceful homeland he was treasuring. In fact, I felt that kind of comfort couldn't last long. Feelings like that didn't belong to Shanghai. They were outside the turbulence of her everyday life, outside my own feelings in this turbulence.

He seemed quite sympathetic, but I was looking at the raincoat hanging against the wall. She had worn it when she had visited me.

"She's gone out shopping for a while, but she'll be back soon."

"Have you quarreled since?"

"Oh—quarreled?" The light vanished from his face. Suddenly he looked pathetically frail. "Yes. Even yesterday, late at night. Eventually she became . . . hysterical. Have you ever seen the face of someone that's hysterical? It's really horrible. The eyes turn up . . . the face gets white as a sheet. It becomes totally transformed. At these

times they forget about . . . being self-conscious. They
shout. Their voices get terribly loud . . . so loud the entire neighborhood can hear. The Chinese living across
the street from us . . . definitely heard her . . . since they
opened their shutters."

"Does she get that way often?"

"Yesterday was really unusual. She was almost like a
savage. When you see it . . . you actually get sick of
human beings. You don't feel hatred, but horror. No
matter how much love or pity you try to feel, you can't,
just at that time only."

There were tears on his cheeks. Letting them fall
calmed him.

"It's impossible to overcome her hysteria . . . unless
you get that way yourself. It's impossible . . . unless you
believe she's not human . . . that she's an animal. And
inevitably that's just how I come to feel. Look where she
scratched me." He pointed to the side of his neck. "She
tried to strangle me. I threw a glass at her and a teacup.
I'd have let her kill me if she wanted to . . . but she didn't
try to go that far. In fact, it would have been a relief . . .
to get rid of all the pain and sadness I've felt. Sometimes
it's unbearable . . . just to be quietly alone with her."

I handed him the towel by his pillow, and I sliced up
another orange. He had only eaten a quarter of his. I
was sucking the juice of my second.

"Sometimes I wondered . . . if she'd kill me. Even
when there wasn't the slightest clue she wanted to . . . I
deliberately tried to think she did. Of course I didn't
have a single thing to go on since she was taking care of
me. Looking after me. And even while I wondered, I
wasn't afraid, perhaps . . . because I'd come so close to
dying anyway. I merely thought she'd have quite a job
if she tried to. Instead of thinking about being killed, I
thought about the effort . . . it takes to kill. It didn't
seem possible . . . anyone could go on living after killing

蝮
の
す
え

47

someone. To be killed is all right, but I couldn't stand the thought . . . of someone hating me that much to do it."

"Does she hate you that much? I doubt it."

"You're right. She doesn't. It's the contempt I have for her that she can't stand. If I stare absentmindedly at the ceiling, she says . . . I'm showing my contempt. It's true that occasionally I've been thinking of her affair with Karajima . . . sometimes even thinking she's so completely satisfied with his body that I can see her performing the act. But I finally end up forgiving her. Pitying her. But she can't believe that. The more silent I am, the more I'm tormenting her . . . she says. She says that in spite of my illness, I'm getting her so nervous with my deceptive silence she can hardly breathe. She claims . . . that's how I'm getting my revenge. True, sometimes I've had that kind of rotten feeling, sometimes getting a real kick out of having tormented her. But more often than not, frankly, I've just about had all the exhaustion I can take. It's humiliating to have to admit it, but I've even tried to forget everything that's happened. Tried to think nothing has. I've even forgiven Karajima. Once I return to Japan, I'll forget everything. Just the two of us will live on together. Erasing everything in our past. It's out of the question they'll allow Karajima to come back. So just the two of us will return . . . to our earlier peaceful years. That's the sort of weak, spineless, resigned state I'm in . . . most of the time. I pass my days in that hazy, quiet way. But she gets annoyed and eventually she's terrible. Like yesterday."

Again he started to talk, but stopped suddenly. A painful expression was on his face. It had really been an effort to come out with these difficult words.

"Yesterday . . . she went shopping for about an hour. She looked awfully ill . . . when she came back. I knew Karajima had got his hands on her. I asked her about it, but she refused to answer. All she said was that nothing was wrong. She boiled some water and prepared supper in the kitchen and brought it in. I tried to help her out ... by talking about our living quietly once we returned, about everyone's suffering because of Japan's defeat, about it being better for those who can rest to take it easy. I even told her ... I was getting to where I could love her again. My mind was getting back to normal, forgetting everything. And then in a joking way, I asked if Karajima hadn't merely done to her what I had. Wasn't it simply ... a trivial act between a man and a woman? Suddenly she glared at me. She had been looking down, crying. All of a sudden she edged up to my pillow ... and straining her voice ... said, 'Let's separate please!' What? I asked. 'Let's separate! Right after we get home!' Did she realize ... what she was asking? All she wanted was for us to separate. She'd get on the ship with me, but once we were home, she'd leave right away. I told her to stop being ridiculous. Hadn't I said ... I'd forget everything ... that we'd begin over again? But she didn't want that. She wanted a separation! Suddenly all I could feel was anger. The anger and pain I was feeling was all I could think about ... when I realized the terrible things she was saying ... to a sick man. I threw the water in my glass at her ... and she stood up. Then I threw my glass and teacup at her. Abandoning me, aren't you? ... I asked. That's right, isn't it! I understand! If you aren't, why begin saying such things. ... when I'm this sick? If you feel that way, get out! Get out of here! She looked at me and threw off her jacket. Suddenly she turned toward me. Her face had already changed ... to something rigid ... as if she were glaring at me. She said ... she'd just slept with Karajima. She pulled off her skirt. She said she hadn't wanted to ... but that he'd come for her in his car. He'd done ... all sorts of things to her. She was

蝮
の
す
え

49

pressing against me from above the covers. She continued shouting out their sexual acts . . . She recklessly let everything be known . . . saying once he'd done it one way, once another. Her weight against me . . . her terrible screams . . . they almost made me faint. I didn't care about the sordid details. But her shrill voice . . . and bloodshot eyes kept terrifying me. The way she exposed her teeth, her hot heavy breath! She began strangling me . . . and screaming, 'A man like you, like you!' I felt something superhuman . . . was attacking me . . . a primitive savage or an ape. Finally her voice got all choked up, her throat heaving, as if she were going to vomit. When she eventually stood up, she slipped on her coat, closed the door, and ran down the steps. I was so exhausted . . . I felt I'd stop breathing any moment. I was trembling so much . . . I thought I was going to pass out. My one regret was that I didn't have the energy to bring her back . . . as she walked through the streets— it's cold at night, you see. I fell asleep . . . crying. When I opened my eyes in the morning, she was changing the ice in my pillow."

For a while I heard loud firecrackers. It seemed as if they had ripped open the dry air.

"She kept herself busy working, as if she'd forgotten all about the night before. I didn't feel like saying anything. We glided over the surface of things with small talk. One step and we might have broken through that surface . . . and the confusion would have been endless. It was as if I'd already lost even the energy to suffer. The physical pain of sickness must be all I can suffer from. Yes, I'd return to Japan. At least she'd probably take me."

The languid sounds of an organ drifted by from the elementary school administered like the temple schools of old. The young girls were singing a melancholy Japanese song, an old one usually sung with the koto. As I listened to the invalid, I felt the profound human link between the sick man and his wife. That painful and intense link of suffering made me an outsider after all, completely separated from them. My own feelings at present were quite uninvolved in comparison. But to be as I was might have meant lack of depth, perhaps merely avoidance of pain. In avoiding pain, I was probably indifferent to it. I wondered if I could escape the consequences of that kind of attitude.

"You better go back to Japan. They say a ship's on its way and will be here within a week."

"Look, Mr. Sugi," the invalid said, his glistening eyes reflecting his feelings. "My wife's been wondering if you'd help us out by going back on the same ship with us."

"On a hospital ship? Is that possible?"

"Maybe. If an invalid's carried into the ship on a stretcher, apparently someone outside the family can go. Please come with us if it's not inconvenient, if you haven't anything to keep you here."

"There's nothing holding me back. It's just that it's useless to return."

"If it's convenient then, come to my home with us. Another thing—" He broke off temporarily, averting his glance by looking at the ceiling. " —My wife. She likes you."

I saw his lips tremble slightly. I remembered the softness of his wife's lips on that rainy day. I had the feeling he already knew about us. When he saw I was going to say something, he said hurriedly, "Lately, that's what she keeps telling me. Just to look at you makes her feel safe. It's an odd thing to say, but don't be offended . . . She really likes you."

"I like her too," I had to say. "I do, because she has some qualities that are just overwhelming."

"Oh you do like her, don't you?" His laugh was thin and weak. That laughing voice went through me far more

蝮
の
す
え

coldly and ominously than his crying voice had. It revealed how close he was to dying.

I knew he was testing me. On the other hand, it was ridiculous to think he was. I was simply embarrassed in a fumbling sort of way. His words, in contrast to mine, were decisive, his voice low like the utterance of a prophecy or prayer.

"The words of the sick before they die are true. They keep thinking about things day and night."

I wanted to respond with something witty. But strong words, clever words, were futile. I merely wanted to conceal how uneasy and agitated I was. Yet that was futile too.

"I don't understand it," I said, "but the two of you and I have ended up in a relationship we can't get out of."

"Yes. You see that, do you? And with Karajima too, you've ended up that way."

I left the invalid before his wife returned.

Outside the New Year celebrating continued. Two men in gaudy red and green costumes were dancing on a riverboat. They looked like the strolling comic dancers we have in Japan. The audience of children, and the men themselves, seemed happy.

When I got home my landlady told me the woman had come. "About an hour after you left. She's quite pretty, that one!"

An artist-friend picked me up in the afternoon. We went out drinking, and instead of going home later, I walked to his house in the suburbs. Some reporters were there for an all-night drinking session.

The next day I toured the outskirts of the city with my friend. I noticed a beer company under British management, boats on the river, the extensive scenery of the desolate winter. Though we were in one of the areas where the Japanese were forced to live, it was far from the city, and the fields and creeks and roads stretched far into the distance under the movement of the vast sky. A long time had passed since I had seen the naked earth and trees in winter colors. It refreshed me to steep myself in them.

The artist was able to make dinner for us after selling a rug in his downstairs room. He got a hot bath ready for me by burning some sliding doors and clapboard. He had already received permission to return home and was merely waiting for notification of his departure. Everyone was talking about repatriation to Japan. Each of the Japanese zones was nervously agitated. In these lonely places in the suburbs, the tension of those returning or remaining was even more intense when they talked about it.

"What are you going to do?"

"I may find myself going back right away," I said. I hadn't forgotten the invalid's request. "But I'm not certain yet. It depends on the way things go."

"It's hard to leave. Shanghai's such a good place."

"It's not a question of good or bad. Somehow I feel I still have things I ought to do." As if warning myself, I had replied carefully. I felt that if I returned without doing something here, I'd have lost a precious chance. I had a premonition of the thrill I would feel in grabbing a heavy lump of truth dirtied with tears and blood. Before I went back, if I hadn't grabbed that unpleasant lump, limp like a pig's guts, it would disappear forever. I had only to take one step forward. And I was probably destined to take just one step more out of bounds. Generally no one has that kind of foreknowledge. But the invalid and his wife knew it, and I did too. Perhaps even Karajima did. With these thoughts in mind, I had been eating slowly, listening to the discussion of art that had been going on. In my drunken state I saw everything around me as charged with meaning. I continued drink-

蝮
の
す
え

53

ing. And as I did, "human existence" revealed itself to me in colors far more thick and sensual than those brilliant touches in my friend's oil painting propped up in the corner. That image of "human existence" surrounded me, threatening me, glittering, making noises, burning in whirls. I decided to hurl myself into it.

I stayed two nights and returned to the city with the reporters in their three-wheeled car. Quite a few Chinese workers in gray overalls were sitting in the street in front of a theatre. The water-drenched asphalt glittered brightly. Pedestrians stepped quickly to the side to avoid the laborers. Twice as many soldiers as usual were opposite the theatre. With their pistols or rifles in hand, they had a murderous expression on their tanned faces. Some Japanese, talking together, looked on from behind an iron gate.

I left the car and went back home. My landlady told me the workers, who hauled lumber from the river, had been out to retrieve a group of laborers arrested by the Security Force. Guns had gone off, and some men had been wounded. I felt as if the stench of violent men and cruel disagreements was closing in on me.

"Right in the middle of everything that woman turned up again. Just when the guns were shooting."

My landlady was annoyed at my having stayed out two nights without notifying her. "She came yesterday and again today. It's a shame! Well, where've you been hanging out?"

She was fanning a fire under a small portable stove. Then, as if remembering something, she suddenly searched through her apron pockets. "By the way, this person showed up," she said, handing me his namecard. It was Karajima's. He had scrawled in pencil some instructions to meet him that night at the Golden Restaurant.

I went up to my room, crept under the bedding I had

left spread out on the mats, and slept for about two hours. My room was cold and damp, and I was tired. I could still feel the jolt of the three-wheeled car as it ran through the streets jammed with excitement. But I was caught up in a calm sweet sleep. I had conceived a pure affection for the invalid's wife. I was gentle, obedient. The radiant, childlike smile on her face was totally innocent. Only the two of us were alive, no one else. Our minds were at rest. To be so much at ease was new for me. I wondered how that was possible. The odors, like those of a midsummer noon, were sweet. "It's all right," she said. "You don't understand? You do!" she said, frowning in her usual way, scolding me gently.

" I understand," I replied, but I really didn't. Then my dream ended. Sitting up in bed, I wondered why we had been so much at ease at that moment. I finally concluded we had probably died.

It was way past my seven o'clock appointment. The Japanese curfew was at eight. In the darkness I hurried to the tavern. The Golden Restaurant was quite small. Most of its customers were Japanese, and I had often gone there. It served cheap tidbits along with sake—beans, radishes, and the like. That was why the newspapermen made it their hangout. Sometimes you even had to stand and wait. But after the New Year even the line of regular customers had thinned out because no one had very much left to sell. That was why the tavern nowadays was deserted. The blank-faced owner and waiters were seen with nothing to do but rest with their hands holding up their chins.

As I pushed open the door and went in, I heard a deep voice shouting. A group of three waiters was looking in. The long tavern was so narrow that walking through was inconvenient. Light brown jugs were stacked to the ceiling on one side, and the remainder of the room had five or so square tables in it. At the innermost table were two

蝮
の
す
え

Japanese quarreling. The one with his back toward me was clearly Karajima. The light kept me from recognizing the other at first, but on looking more closely, I saw it was Aoki. Karajima had grabbed the smaller man by the neck and was pressing him against the edge of a table. Aoki's small dark face had lost its color. Aoki, who was a born fighter, was making as much fuss as a child, his face as twisted as if he'd been crying.

"Maybe you think you've beaten me, but I won't admit to defeat by force!"

"By what then?"

Karajima's large, radiant profile was alive with arrogance. He turned in my direction. For the first time I noticed his shoulders and waist under the leather jacket he was wearing were really quite large. "All of you talk big, but you good-for-nothing bastards can't do a thing. What's there to win by if not by force? I'm busy. Get going."

After pulling Aoki close to him, Karajima shoved him toward the entrance. He bumped into tables and chairs and staggered toward the group of waiters. Then he fell backwards on the floor, but got up immediately. Grabbing one of the bottles of wine lined along the counter, Aoki screamed, "Bastard!" and again rushed at Karajima. The raised bottle was violently warded off, striking a wall and shattering. Some drops of wine landed on my face. Karajima, his own face red, grabbed Aoki by the shoulders and easily lifted him. With his feet flapping in the air, Aoki was thrown through the entrance and out into the street. All that time Karajima hadn't looked at me or the waiters. As he went back to his seat, his face was tense yet sullen. He sat down so violently his enormous body made his chair squeak. Noticing Aoki's hat on the table, he hurled it toward the waiters. His blunt "Take that!" sounded as if the waiters were inanimate, as if he were flinging a dog a bone.

"Warm some sake!" Karajima demanded, but the next moment, after rearranging his chopsticks and other things that had been upset, he tried to soften his expression. Then he offered me a seat.

On the table were many expensive side-dishes glittering with oil, dishes I had never been able to order. He poured some wine into his own cup from the lead bottle the waiter had brought him. "Lousy!" Karajima said after tasting a drop. He told the waiter to bring him something else. Karajima's way of speaking not only revealed his contempt for the waiter but indicated how the man was considered less than human. Karajima's words contained the extreme of indifference, as if he were flattening the waiter with a flyswatter. Once, during the war, a similar act of Karajima's at a publishers' convention had annoyed me. He had mounted the platform and had deliberately leered out at the gathered faces. Then he extended his arm to point to someone seated in a certain row. "Who are you?" Karajima had demanded. The youth, seventeen or eighteen, had apparently been sent to sit in during an interval one of the publishers couldn't attend. The substitute became thoroughly confused.

"Get out of here! Right away! Punks like you wouldn't understand even if you can listen! Get out!" Karajima looked as if he were about to spit or do something worse. He began his speech in a threatening tone, "The Japanese spirit . . ." Already he had forgotten his rebuke to the young man. Even the action of scolding, Karajima refused to acknowledge as an act. He exuded the self-confidence that he and the young man were totally separate, that the existence of persons not to Karajima's taste was not to be allowed. How I had hated the power behind his self-confidence, the eloquence of his speech, the authority he represented. I had felt his kind of individuality was phony, merely the dark, hopeless, reverse side of authority. Yet I had thought I myself was

蝮

の

す

え

weaker than an insect, someone who couldn't even touch that authority with the tip of a finger.

But now, right in front of me, sat Karajima, who had lost his influence. If I felt hatred for him, it was for his individuality, not for the authority he had represented.

"Nice of you to come," he said, greedily munching on some roast pork and shrimp. "I know quite well the contempt you have for me."

When I emptied my cup, he filled it immediately.

"Please help yourself. You don't want to? Don't you want to enjoy my hospitality?"

I tried one of the delicacies. It dissolved at the tip of my tongue, spread over my entire mouth, and pleasantly disappeared down my throat.

He chuckled and smiled slightly. "You're interesting. I've always thought so." His sly, sharp eyes were feeling me out. "What's your opinion of me? I mean of me as a man?"

". . . During the war I didn't feel you were human. I hadn't the slightest interest in you. Recently, though, I have."

"How come?"

". . . Because of her, of course." I deliberately spoke as if it were troublesome to. He put down his chopsticks, emptied his cup, filled it again.

"You've heard everything? She's told you everything? Well. What do you think of my mistress?"

My face indicated I didn't want to talk about it.

". . . All right, if you don't want to tell me. Well, drink up!" He brought his face close to mine in the anxiously overpolite manner of a man with a trick up his sleeve. His skin had a quite healthy glow.

"What was all that about with Aoki?" I asked.

"Aoki? The bastard came in while I was drinking and sat himself down at a table near the entrance. He had the nerve to bitch in a low voice if I was still 'pissing around.' I kept warning him. He's a coward, you know, but he still does a lot of talking.''

"He's probably not the only one surprised you're still 'pissing around.' "

Karajima came out with an angry crude look, but immediately returned to his pose of deliberately being nonchalant. The way he licked his lips, oily from the pork, you'd have thought he was trying to keep something nauseous from sticking in his throat.

"That's right! It's not just Aoki. All you bastards feel that way. All of you complain like feeble women. You know you'd be better off if I died. But not one of you bastards is brave enough to put me out of the way. Aoki's a punk, but at least he's stupidly frank. He challenged me even though he hasn't any physical strength. But you could see what he really was when he was working in the Rice Control Agency. He ran his ass off for the company tormenting the hell out of the Chinese by monopolizing the sale of rice. He was inefficient, stupid, scared. You can sum him up by saying he was being used, that he could never be in a position to use others. No matter what he does, he hasn't the power to control men. The way I see it, whether he lives or dies, his existence means nothing. How I despise bastards like him! But I won't allow them to despise me. I guess they'll charge me with war crimes. Maybe the Chinese government will throw the book at me. But you bastards can't. You never will. Understand? Never."

He came out with a slight laugh. Rather than call it an impudent laugh, I found it dismally profound.

"The way you bastards live is also meaningless. For the most part, you're penniless. Your retirement pay gets you nowhere. Each day prices are doubling. The best you can do is sponge off the crumbs of Chinese merchants and bank presidents. Guys come in for handouts even from me! I've some gold bars I've put away. If I dispose of them one at a time, I'll be able to enjoy myself for two or three years. If I deposit them with a few Chinese moneylenders, the interest alone will support me comfortably for the rest of my life. You heard about that Japanese who worked for the Chinese Railway and wrote some nonsense about dying of starvation, didn't you? A jerk writing that kind of stuff won't die like that in a million years. If you're dying of starvation, you starve in a corner somewhere without saying anything about it. First of all, what's the good of a real man stupidly announcing his own worthlessness by talking of starving to death? If he wants to die like that, why not? I've no money to hand over to bastards that want to go on living by capitalizing on death by starvation. Let them rail at me, hate me. They're free to. But what the hell can they do? Since they're weak, they're weak. That's all there is to it. Let them rationalize if they want to. But go anywhere in the world and you see that it's useless to rationalize. At any rate, I've my own power. They had none from the beginning. They're just ghosts that have nothing to do with money, with power— No matter how much they may have wanted to seize power, the fact remains they haven't been able to. I've lost my authority. Now I'm definitely the underdog. There's no comparing myself to what I was before. But the authority I had I got by my own strength. Do you see? Understand? That power remains in me undiminished!"

I found his words more plausible than his wartime speeches. But the voice was the same. His strident insistence hadn't changed. I briefly glanced at the waiters. Sometimes looking outside, sometimes wiping tables, they seemed to say, without revealing it on their faces, that the damn Japs were arguing again.

"That's enough. I don't want to hear anymore. I was fed up enough listening to your wartime crap."

My voice was comparatively quiet. The initial excitement had passed. The force of his conviction made me even wearier, more depressed.

"That's just like you. Always sarcastic. That's all you're good for."

"That's not all," I said.

"Not all? Well, then, what are you going to do?"

"I may be a weakling. But I don't feel you've any monopoly on power. You're not so different from me, are you?"

"No?" he said, laughing in finding me either contemptible or pathetic. "You mean I'm no different from any of you bastards? No? You're welcome to think so if you want. What a sweet guy you are! Me, in a few days from now I'm going to take her to the French Settlement and hide out there. I'll take her even if I have to drag her. I'll let you in on something. I don't have much longer to live. I've no regrets about that. But what I want to do I do. I'm in love with her. I really am. I'm not handing her over to anyone while I'm alive. Even if she hates me. She does already. She did from the first. But even while hating me, I probably gave her enough satisfaction. Now, though, it's different. She's changed. She keeps talking about some stupid nonsense that I don't have anything spiritual in me the way you have. Maybe that's how it is— But I can't give her up. That's why I'm locking her up."

"Do you think you can get away with it?"

"I haven't the slightest doubt about that. I still have four or five men working for me." He had the shrewd look of a detective or an MP or a public prosecutor. All over that magnificent face of his with its imposing features was an expression that easily and customarily subjugates the opposition.

"Some foreigners can help me hide out in the Settlement. I invited you today just to let you know. And depending on the circumstances, I intended to kill you.

蝮
の
す
え

61

That's the truth. Even now I have that intention. And you probably came suspecting that. I had a feeling you did the minute I turned around while I was knocking the hell out of Aoki and I saw you come in. I'm a real expert on intuition. Besides, I'm not a fool. When I saw you come in, I thought of an honor student in elementary school boldly venturing forth to the home of the class troublemaker."

"And I thought of you as a high school bully picking on a freshman."

We laughed at the same time and stopped just as soon. For me the situation was tense and awkward. It annoyed me to find I was becoming too serious. Somehow I felt confused and couldn't think straight. The humiliation of this face-to-face meeting and its uselessness confused me. It embarrassed me not to know what to do. That was why I couldn't become violent. If I couldn't hate him, that meant he wasn't on my mind. I wondered if I hadn't already stopped thinking about him.

"During the war I acted the gentleman. There's no need to anymore. To use a favorite phrase of you bastards—'to be other than myself' is no longer necessary. Go on laugh. Sure I lectured on the Japanese spirit. So often that people got fed up listening, like you said. But they did believe in my speeches and they died. My younger brothers died. The dead won't come back again. Definitely won't—"

He was drunker than I was. His large arms made the table shake.

"They can't return! Even in dreams! They're forgotten! At first slowly, then completely! What do you think of this kind of world? Even with all that crap about the Japanese spirit, I go on living. Even today I'm living! And even if you can live quite well without the Japanese spirit, I gave speeches that made those that didn't have it traitors! Bastards that took those speeches at face value and joyfully believed in them and died! Sure, there were other jerks like you and Aoki and her. What the hell's this bitch of a Japan that's made up of me and bastards like that? Well, what is it? Let them punish me with death. That's divine justice. And if it's not, it's all right too. It's retribution. In a nutshell, it's the world's retribution. Sure . . . okay with me. But even if they punish me, nothing'll be settled. Nothing. I'll be reborn. Perhaps as a Japanese. I won't be any South Sea native. Probably not even a Frenchman. Because I'm different. Racially different. It's better if they exterminate us Japanese. Exterminated or not, we won't get away without paying for it. That's impossible. The problem won't end with a reluctant smile. It won't end with sarcasm. Better watch out! Even you intellectuals are involved!"

He stretched out the ending of "intellectuals." That pleased him, and he repeated the word several times.

"Intellectuals, the conscience of the world! Right, ain't it? Maybe getting involved nauseates you, but it's your responsibility. Still, not one of you intellectuals will be able to become the arms and legs and stomachs and intestines of society! The best you can be is its nerves. Nagging nerves fit for the scrap heap! You Japanese intellectuals, what's more, are the nerve-endings of a strange and ridiculous race. Even if you get your nerves up, you're useless. Not one of us, not the world either, feels any vibration from you. To strain the metaphor, we're the blood-pumpers. When we want to stop, we stop. Stop at our own sweet will! You can't stop even if you want to!"

I kept eating the fried pork and shrimp and green peas, and I kept on drinking. Apart from what he was saying, I gradually noticed in the urgency with which he rattled on a seriousness of a different kind from his former eloquence, the seriousness of a man driven into a corner, squeezing out his almost breathless voice, cursing. It

蝮のすえ

63

seemed to me he had reached the end of life. His cursing of the intellectuals didn't matter. What mattered to me was the force he was about to use on his mistress. I wondered if I had the nerve to speak about that. Despite all he had said, wasn't he really lonely? Now that she was his one hope, wasn't it loneliness to take by force what despised him? He derided the weak, but was he ultimately any stronger? Wasn't his strength merely the simplicity of derision, the sweetness of desperation? I tried framing these words, but I stopped. I had satisfied my hunger, and I was drunk and tired. To repeat what he had said, it's useless to rationalize, no matter what the situation. I no longer had any need to listen to his coercive words.

"I'm going home. How about giving me your address?" I said. He wrote it down and made a rough map on the back of his namecard.

"In any event, I'm taking her with me in a few days and disappearing!" he said forcefully. "Go on, interfere. But it'll be useless. You seem serious. More serious than I thought. But seriousness isn't the least useful. Pity, isn't it? Yes, it's true. You damn well better not come up with any fancy Japanese spirit!"

Bumping against tables and chairs, he saw me to the entrance.

"It just may be I'll kill you. Trivial perhaps, but unavoidable. You know, there are times when power becomes uncontrollable. See, I'm never serious. I—"

I went out the door the waiter held open for me. Karajima's voice vanished into the cold wind. Only the red charcoal from a soup stall on the street and the steam from the pots looked warm. Not a single Chinese, much less a Japanese, was to be seen. The only place with any life in the deadly silent surroundings was a recently opened bar. I was really beginning to feel drunk. Perhaps because of the moon and stars, the streets were brighter than when I had first come out. "We're nerves, you say?"

I was walking unsteadily. "Just the nerve-endings of a strange and ridiculous race, you say? We can't even stop? Can't? Is that possible? We have to pay for it? Can't expect to get off scot-free? That's it! But the bastard'll kill me? Right! The main point above everything else. The heart's going to kill the nerves then. What for? Why?"

A bike brushed my sleeve and went off after almost colliding with me. The rider turned back to swear at me in Chinese. "The heart—the nerves? What the hell we doing?"

I raised my hands over my head. I saw my shadow fall on the asphalt as if a gorilla had just started walking. I deliberately bent my knees, and waving my hands above my head, I did a gorilla walk along the alley.

Three uniformed police were coming from the opposite direction. Their shoes sounded in unison. Their gold numerals glittered on their fresh blue collars.

"Hey! Cut that out. Can't do that," one of them said, mimicking me, gently rebuking me. "You Japanese?" the others said, peering at me. They walked off when I lowered my hands. Once they were out of sight, I again lifted my hands and bent my knees. Shadows from a row of tall shop buildings, their doors fastened ominously, darkened the entire street. I swaggered with each step planted firmly on the ground, and I walked through the darkness of overlapping shadows. I walked like a monster of superior physical strength emerging from the forest to the spot where blood was to be spilled. I was overflowing with confidence as if I were anyone but myself, a magnificent beast whose power went beyond mere nerves. Already the caution of the good citizen who lowers his head and obeys regulations had vanished.

蜊
の
す
ゑ

THE NEXT DAY we crossed Garden Bridge. She had kept badgering me to, but I had also felt like taking a walk on the other side of the river. It was out-of-bounds for the Japanese, so we had removed our armbands. It had been a long while since we had last seen the streetcars, bikes, and rickshaws slowly mounting the steeply arched iron bridge so elevated at the center. Along the edge of the river rolled the yellow waves. I seemed to be trying to recapture the past, so greedily did I take in the trivial views of our former consulate, the junks and warships, the various national flags astir in the breeze. Up to the end of the war we had lived in the French Settlement, so now we hated the filthy streets of our district. As we walked, she joyfully held on to my arm. In the morning sun were brand-new cars and jeeps speedily racing along the road beside the river. So painfully dazzling was their speed that I saw the two of us as outcasts in this bright world of motion.

The police and street-vendors kept staring at her. That didn't restrain her—she was so buoyant over being liberated.

"Where have you been having such a good time the last two days? I was worried because I didn't know if you were hiding out."

Not a bit concerned about the congestion around her, she had begun talking about herself. A narrow but long park had been built along the Bund. We sat down on one of the benches facing the river. We stretched our legs on the railing before us. Although it was an ordinary railing, it was quite thick and long, but so solid that it almost looked ridiculous. Yet merely seeing it along the Bund made me feel the tremendous power of the British Empire. I found it strange that the mere thickness of a piece of iron I hadn't even noticed until the end of the war seemed ample evidence of a power that was beyond coping with.

"We've permission to take a passenger. So even if you don't really want to, come back with us on the hospital ship. If you disappear when it's time to embark, I'll be quite annoyed!"

"I'll go if I can."

"If you can?"

"What about Karajima?"

"Don't worry about him. Once we're on board, it's over. Are you worried? Don't be since I'll take care of him."

"Is he that easy to handle?"

"Karajima? There's nothing we can do about him. You see that, don't you? Instead of worrying about him, concentrate on not changing your mind about leaving!"

Repatriation wasn't as light a matter with me as it apparently was with her. There was still the question of what Karajima was going to do. I imagined something bloody. That consideration aside, it was impossible for me to simply detach myself suddenly from Shanghai and return home. To go back to the Japan of old and to abandon the complexities of my Shanghai days would be cause for regret. I'd merely settle down. I doubted if I could look forward to any change, development, fear, desire.

"What's on your mind?"

"Something tells me I don't want to go back," I said.

"I know. I don't want to either."

A lingering puff of white smoke from a steamship drifted along the surface of the wide river. Some children around the bench next to ours looked eagerly down at the yellow waves dashing against the wharf below. Someone, perhaps a clerk, was leaning on the bench and idly watching the river. A few spectators stood up to leave. It suddenly occurred to me that these Chinese citizens, these men and women, knew nothing about such places

蝮
の
す
ゑ

67

as Japan. Most of them would never see Japan, and for the first time I realized that the two of us were foreigners linked together by our land. The clerk and those children were on a routine excursion to the park along the river. That was what they had come to see. But their geography ended there. At the proper time they would go back to their company or department store or tenement building. They would return to colleagues or families. But we were leaving Shanghai quite soon, never to return a second time. Perhaps our ship was already on the river. These thoughts, so filled with subjective meaning, made the scenes on the river close in on me.

"I thought we might hide out in the French Settlement. We'd be happy if we could."

"That's impossible," I said.

"But if we could, wouldn't we be happy?"

Her suddenly bringing up the French Settlement, as Karajima had, worried me. It was perfectly obvious she was as desperate as Karajima. Not only that. I couldn't believe in happiness. Cohabiting couldn't bring happiness. I was convinced that whatever was stable collapsed in time. I had never anticipated that happiness could materialize. Certainly the warmth of her happiness might be transmitted to me if we tried it. But I knew that possibility no longer appealed to me. It all boiled down to the fact that I was more familiar, more secure, with unhappiness. Something artificial in the word "happiness" itself lay behind her own use of the term.

"Oh I want to be happy!" she said.

"Can living with me make you happy?"

She was confident it could.

A clear indication of the unhappiness attached to the word itself was in the fact that someone in as precarious a position as hers, someone in the midst of danger, was all the more committed to happiness.

"I heard how bad your recent attack of hysteria was."

"What? Heard about it? I don't even know what I did." Her face looked lonely and embarrassed. It was delicate and lovely.

"You must have been quite disgusted with me after hearing about it."

"Not at all. For the first time I realized how justifiably beyond human control hysteria is."

"Then you did understand! You probably pitied me."

She took my hand and gripped my fingers and rubbed them with her hands. She seemed to enjoy caressing me in that old-fashioned, reserved way.

"A little while ago I asked you to protect me. That's all over. You don't have to."

"Why not?"

"Oh why! I also asked you to kill Karajima, didn't I? That's over too. Don't think about killing. You don't have to protect me with all your might! All you have to do is love me! Think of nothing else. Don't get involved anymore with Karajima. I tell you I'm worried. If anything should happen to you—if you should be killed, anything!"

She turned to me with that special look she used before her tears fell. She glanced down and wiped her eyes with her fingers. I held those fingers.

"It's nothing for Karajima to put you out of the way. So no matter what he writes, don't go to see him."

I hadn't yet told her of our meeting. I hadn't told her about his behavior, his words, the resolution he had revealed at the end of our talk. Possibly she knew already. She had a premonition of danger. And it was even stronger since she knew more about Karajima than I did. She was trying to protect me, at least trying to make me avoid any possible involvement. And I could have avoided it if I had felt like it. Obviously, as long as I didn't try to meet him again, things would pass without incident. But I felt that was impossible. If the event merely

蝮
の
す
ゑ

69

passed away without anything happening to me, that would mean I was an absolute zero. She'd be taken by force to the French Settlement, and the invalid would be left alone. Preventing this had nothing to do with justice. I didn't believe in justice. But I had become conscious of the fact that my withdrawal meant I'd become a nonentity. On meeting Karajima the night before, I was still only vaguely antagonistic. But my fear of being reduced to a zero was so very clear to me now that it was as if I had only just become conscious of the implications. As long as I lived by maintaining that fear, I couldn't become a nonentity. I had thought of myself as merely existing. But I now found that even in that state one inevitably has form and substance. When I held her fingers, moist from her tears, that awareness was physically represented to me through those fingers. I was surprised to find myself rejecting the possibility of becoming a zero. The tension I felt was as sharp as sitting down in ice cold water. Before I realized it, I was telling myself I could be killed and that even if I were, I deserved it. In a flash I realized I had decided my own destiny.

"I'd die if anything happened to you." Her large eyes were moist with tears.

I had never thought I'd hear such pathetic and dramatic words from a woman. Nor had I ever thought *she* would say them. I hadn't even known anyone could casually come out with such words.

"I wouldn't mind dying then," she said.

She laughed lightly. "Really, I wouldn't."

I recalled the words of a senior who had once told me of the frequency with which women use the word "die." Her profile after its earlier childlike radiance was now shrouded in the moodiness of the aged. Appropriate to this transformation, comparable to that of flower gardens in violent storms, her words gave the impression she was really ready to die. And those words, like a silhouette or an odor or a nuance that was beautifying her, had escaped through her lips and seeped through me.

"Leave it to me. It'll work out all right." She had suddenly returned to reality, had suddenly become businesslike.

"I know some men. Koreans and Chinese. If I ask them, they'll help me out one way or another. So don't worry. We'll be able to get back fairly soon."

All at once her earlier cheerfulness returned. It was genuinely spontaneous. Already I couldn't keep up with her mood.

Later she said she was meeting Karajima that evening. He had sent her a letter. In it he had informed her he'd be hiding out for a while and would give her all his ready cash. He had designated the time and place.

"It's probably a lie," I said at once.

"Not necessarily. That's the least he ought to do for me."

"But don't go," I said as if reprimanding her. For a moment she was silent, as though she were thinking it over.

"I won't go if you're worried. And if I don't, you shouldn't go to see him either. All right? Good! I'll have someone go for me tonight."

"Is there someone that can?"

"I think so."

"But it's not really necessary, is it? Just ask the Security Division to have someone stay at your house. Don't go out. In the first place, you're too careless. Don't even come to me. I'll go to your place. Don't go out at all until they call for the passengers to board."

She nodded obediently.

I took her back. On the way she said, "If only you hadn't started copying documents, you wouldn't be in this mess," and she laughed. Her words really struck home.

When I got to my place, I found two Chinese workmen removing steam pipes from the kitchen and my room. They were making quite a racket as they also took off the closet doors and carried them downstairs. Since my landlord had become ill at the end of the year, he had to sell junk of that kind. For the remainder of the day, in the middle of the dust from the demolished wall and the noise of separating the iron pipes and the boards, I continued copying at my crate. One of my jobs involved an old woman who desperately wanted permission to bring her electro-massage to Japan. Another of my clients, a factory owner, was being bothered by the demands of an official in spite of having completed the confiscation proceedings with another government clerk. It grew dark out while I was getting these headaches and others into documentary form.

I had the feeling she might go to meet Karajima that night. In spite of her words, it was a possibility. It was more than that judging from her character. I felt everything would be over between us if she did. The darker it became outside, the stronger grew my premonition. Finally, I had no more doubts about it. It hadn't been my intention to go after she had promised not to. But now that I was certain she would, I was forced into going too. I still had the faint but persistent feeling that I ought to save myself the trouble, that I ought to leave everything as it was. But in order to destroy that feeling too, I had to go tonight.

I imagined that as she was taking care of her sick husband, she was making the same kind of mental preparations I was. Lights on, supper finished, the small talk over. She was inventing some excuse or another, trying to leave. The invalid was suspicious. She sat down, stood up again. I imagined the meaningful passage of time, meaningful for her and for him. I was so tortured by these images that I could feel the pain in my guts.

Once Aoki had said to me, "Your room's just like Raskolnikov's in *Crime and Punishment*. He stole out with an axe. And he got back secretly without anyone recognizing him."

I glanced around my narrow, dark, miserable room. The dismantling that day had made the naked walls even uglier. The ceiling stains from the rain were dark yellow, shaped like foetuses without hands, their legs extended. There was only my dirty bedding except for sake bottles, carbon and writing paper, brushes and inkstone, several books. Yet as long as I was in my room, I had been able to carry out my daily tasks. To go out now would change everything beyond recognition. I lacked Raskolnikov's strong and resilient philosophy. My plan of action was no more than a childish impulse. Furthermore, I didn't have his minute calculation or cool preparation. Above all, I didn't have his depth. I was too dependent and impulsive. I could convince myself that if I went, things would work out somehow. But I didn't have the determination to work them out or do so at any cost even. I hadn't even thought about a weapon yet. "If only you hadn't started copying documents, you wouldn't be in this mess," she had said and laughed. She had spoken out of kindness. But it was the painful truth. After all, I did copy documents. I did them on request. That was how I made money. I was never serious myself. My customers were the only ones involved. I wasn't a hero. I was a bystander's bystander. When I recalled these things, I felt the task ahead of me slipping away in a flash, and I felt dizzy in trying to catch hold of it, my feet shaking, my power failing me.

I picked up a knife that had tumbled down by my books. Its blade was only four inches long. Its broken handle was wound with string. The face I saw reflected on the cold blade had an expression of absurdity rather than one of tragic seriousness.

蝮
の
す
え

"An axe!" My landlady had one to cut firewood for her small portable stove. The size would be convenient. When I went down, if she wasn't there, I would hide the axe in my overcoat pocket. First I put in the knife. Suddenly I remembered its make. *Chrysanthemum*. My younger sister had bought it for me. I recalled her face as if seeing it in a snapshot close up. It remained fixed, smiling. For the first time since coming to Shanghai, I had caught an image of my sister's face. I sensed that she probably intended to protect me. And I felt she might be able to.

No one was in the kitchen. The lights were on in my landlady's room, but it was quiet there. She opened the glass door and looked out. "Can you get me some medicine? Anything for a fever will do." She took some bills from her purse. "Drinking today too? Please come back soon," she said, entering her room and sliding the door shut. Quickly I picked up the axe from the box of charcoal and slipped the weapon into my overcoat pocket. I opened the kitchen door and went out.

The heavy axe was quite bulky. Its shape stuck out taut and hard so that it could certainly be observed under my thick coat. If Karajima noticed, he'd be on guard and would have an added incentive for murdering me. Not to use it would really be idiotic. My own unpreparedness and incompetence exasperated me. But my one hope lay in the axe. I was conscious of every man in the street at night, of every man loitering about. And each time I passed someone, I imagined the moment of raising the axe, of striking out. I'd cut at the flesh of one of these men, strike at his bones, spill his blood—these images so troubled me that slowly and steadily I felt the sweat seeping out of me. I actually was no more than a bundle of nerves. I felt I was walking in order to be killed. The appointed rendezvous spot was near a streetcar line beyond the Chinese residential area far past the shopping district. I stayed in the shadows of the houses on one side.

Suddenly from second-story windows and from doorways yellow lights fell over my entire body. Then darkness again. I merely hurried on to my destination as if I'd forgotten the desperate situation of meeting Karajima, contending with him.

All at once, about thirty feet ahead of me, I heard a loud voice laughing. And then a Japanese said something. Then that laughing voice again. The two men were together. They were heading in the same direction I was and were walking slowly. One was definitely Karajima.

"That so? The wine was bad? I never thought it would be. I took the mud off the jug and opened it myself." Karajima's voice was as clear as ever.

"But it was tasteless," his companion said in a low voice. "It's a shame a man like you should end up drinking such stuff."

"Cut the crap! Something went wrong with the sake, not with me!" They laughed cheerfully.

At first I wondered if Karajima's companion was a subordinate. But apparently Karajima had simply met him on the way. At the next crossing they separated. They had proceeded along that street and then Karajima had turned right. "Give my regards to your wife," he had said and, glancing at his watch, had walked off quickly. He looked resolute, bursting with self-confidence. His proudly squared shoulders seemed especially large that night. I imagined him confronting me with his pompous and detached attitude. If I panicked for a fraction of a second even, it would be as deadly as if my entire body had been shattered. I decided to go on to my destination by proceeding one block ahead of the street he had turned on.

A deserted lot was at the end of the street I took. The scrap iron accumulated by the Japanese army was still piled up high there and enclosed by a rusty barbed wire fence. No one was in the vicinity. At that hour in the

蝮
の
す
え

neighborhood, no Japanese would have been out. So when I reached the corner of the street, Karajima and I would have recognized one another despite the distance between us.

Near the end of the street, the lot, brightened a little by the moon, came into view. It was a peaceful night. Suddenly, from a fairly isolated spot, I heard gravel trampled underfoot. At the same time I heard light footsteps running at great speed, someone falling heavily to the ground.

I ran so fast the bones in my legs snapped. The axe was in my hand. Before I realized it, I was shouting out of breath, "Bastard!" I ran toward a shadow on a caved-in wall. Karajima rose toweringly to his feet. Until then he had been lying on the ground. With his face a grotesque mask of pain, he began grabbing at me. I swung my axe. It cut through the air. The second time it plunged deeply into his body somewhere. He caught hold of me. But what actually happened was that his heavy body had collided with mine, leaning against me. That caused me to fall violently, Karajima's body pinning me down. My head and the palms of my hands touched the cold ground. I struggled to get away. Then Karajima's body slid heavily away from on top of me. I jumped to my feet. Karajima was moaning. I was searching for my axe. He remained where he had fallen. He was lying face down. He twisted his body in jerks and starts. For the first time I could clearly see his face. A white face, a handsome face, but totally transformed from its usual appearance. Oily, lifeless. Exceedingly tense. Almost deranged. He was trying to stand up. I readied my axe, and when he had just about half-risen, I struck at the back of his neck. He fell face forward.

That was when I saw the knife in his back, a razor-sharp, long and slender knife used for cutting meat. It had gone through his coat, piercing his heart or lungs.

That was why he couldn't shout or fight. Someone had already wounded him fatally before I had started my attack.

I couldn't do anything. I couldn't even bear to hold the axe in my hand. I hadn't the energy to fight or hate. The blood streamed out of Karajima's lacerated neck. From that spot alone the blood was spilling out over the ground. His face was twisted toward me. He was looking up at me. His pathetic eyes were terror-stricken, like a dog's, desperately pleading. He had been trying to pull out the knife. He kept attempting to, but had finally looked up at me. He wanted me to do it for him. Before I realized it, I had grabbed the black handle. I pulled it out with all my might. That was all I could have done at the time. Every limb of mine was exhausted, severely chilled. At my feet was a man I knew quite well, a man covered with blood, a man I had talked to only the night before. Afraid, trembling, I had only the urge to cry out or run away.

His eyes closed, then opened. Not the slightest trace of hatred was on his face. There was only fear. That fragile face was full of misery. The flesh on its cheeks contracted spasmodically. The color of his lips changed. They were distorted, apart. He called out her name in a low, inaudible voice, but I felt it had been uttered with a grotesque explosion. He kept calling it. I was bewildered by the fact that he was dying and that I was the only one watching him, that at the end he had called for her but I was the only one listening.

He was lying in agony on the cold mud I myself had been pushed onto a while back. If the assassin had not jabbed a butcher knife deep into Karajima's body, I would have probably been the corpse on that ground. Some water was flowing along the ground. It was gushing out from a conduit that had been left open close by. Some light was reflected on the brass faucet while the water gushed out, and the falling water, itself reflecting light, drenched the barbed wire and scrap iron and gravel.

I left without making certain Karajima had died.

Like Raskolnikov I washed the blood off my weapon. I scoured the axe and the butcher knife with sand and washed them again. Then I put them in my overcoat pockets and went back. I had wanted to rush to her as soon as I could, to find my way to her room where she and her sick mate were lying quietly awake in bed thinking about Karajima and me. Now the two of them were indispensable for me. I needed them to call out to me, to reveal their concern about my whereabouts, to help me in any way they could. But I had decided instead to return to my room. It gave me quite a jolt to see how absorbed I was in saving my own neck. Before I realized it, I was behaving as if I had to establish proof that I had nothing to do with Karajima's murder. Even the slightest suspicion was an apprehension comparable to the destruction of the universe!

"He's already dead. Already cold and stiff." At home, safely in bed, I repeated those words many times. But I continually dreamed he wasn't dead, not quite. My undershirt was soaked through. I kept sweating almost until dawn. I would feel hot, then cold. The sweat would be gone, then come again.

That day I walked in the rain to her house. It was past noon. On the way I heard some Japanese talking about Karajima's murder. Everyone already knew about it. "Just think. Someone with the guts to do a beautiful job like that!" "Was he Japanese or Chinese?" "I bet it was a thief." They were talking about it that casually. I had no idea who the real murderer was. I was so overwrought, so depressed by my experience, I had no energy for any kind of speculation.

"You're safe," she said, running down the steps and

taking both my hands. "I thought you'd come! I bought some wine to celebrate!"

"You know, don't you?"

"Of course! I heard about it when I went shopping this morning."

"Did you really stay home last night?"

"Of course. Why?"

Her composure irritated me. It was so totally out of keeping with my own desperation. "I went out," I said in a serious, moody voice.

"I knew you had the instant I saw you come in. It's written all over your face. Did you kill him?"

"No."

"Who then?"

"I don't know."

"You were there, weren't you? Why don't you know then?"

"I struck him with an axe. But someone else killed him. I don't know who. At any rate, someone stabbed him before I could."

"My husband's been saying you did it. I thought so too."

"But I didn't."

"It doesn't matter. Who cares who it was so long as someone did it!" She hugged me then, kissing me violently. "Now we're safe! Everything's fine now!"

She was pleased, radiant. I was depressed, uneasy, as if my hands were still dirty from the blood, as if I could still hear Karajima moaning. Not even her lips could bring me any relief. Everything was ugly, useless. I was too annoyed even to speak.

As she had indicated, the invalid was convinced I had killed Karajima. No matter what I said to the contrary, all he could do was smile his denial. He even thanked me with tears in his eyes. He was deeply moved. "Forgive me," he pleaded, "for making you do it." And he said,

"You're a great man." I grew silent, merely drinking the wine his wife had prepared. I found it tasteless. I was feeling more and more depressed.

"How did he die?" the invalid asked.

"It wasn't the Karajima we knew. He was afraid, a coward."

"I see. Frightened, you say?"

"Like a child or an idiot. He was so miserable it was painful to look at him. What's more, he kept calling your wife's name."

When I said that, she looked up sharply. "That's a lie! A lie!" She spoke so intensely it made her husband glance back violently.

"I've no reason to lie."

"Well, it's annoying to hear he called my name. I can't believe it." The look of ill-humor she made was the same one has in brushing away a bug clinging to the body.

"He plagues me even after he's dead."

The invalid ignored his wife and began talking to me.

"When I heard the news this morning, all my energy suddenly collapsed. I felt . . . it would now be all right to die. I felt . . . my life was worthwhile . . . just to have heard the news. But as the excitement wore off, I gradually realized that everything was over, that I didn't have anything to wait for any longer. I was vacantly listening to my wife. Karajima . . . no longer existed. His life didn't have the slightest connection to ours anymore. The man that had dominated us up to now, hovering over us day and night like some demon, had, in a flash, ceased to be. That was the strange, empty feeling I was absorbed in. You see, I kept thinking I hadn't done it, that you had, that you had killed him while I had been lying in bed without moving a muscle! I thought of how irresponsible . . . and dependent . . . and sly it was of me . . . to have had you do it. I had suffered, but it was no more than that. I hadn't done a single thing. I had been trying to evade . . . as much as possible, trying to forget . . . as much as possible . . . trying to resign myself. My only thought was to get back to Japan. To be perfectly honest . . . I didn't think you had that much courage. And not merely you. I didn't feel a single man in Shanghai could kill him. I had hoped someone would. But I had believed that was absolutely impossible. Yet I woke up to find it done. But even though I had realized my one desire, it struck me unexpectedly . . . confusing me. I was overjoyed at being freed and revenged, but at the same time I was full of self-pity and shame. I wondered if it was right . . . to allow a human being to be killed . . . for the sake of a man like me, lying in bed, unable to do anything, dependent, irresponsible, a sly, selfish cripple! I wondered if a murder committed for me ought to satisfy me. I began crying, some sort of intensely painful tormenting thing full of shame and regret . . . all of a sudden coming over me. When I told my wife about it, she said Karajima had been trying to kill us, to kill her, you. But if we hadn't been miserable, if I hadn't been a cripple . . . unable to move, you wouldn't have had any trouble. I don't want to remain a cripple! I don't want the shame . . . of being dependent on others! I want to get well! To behave responsibly! I want to do . . . what I have to do, like you, at least once!"

His words were too much for me to take. His crying voice had never disturbed me as much as it did then. I felt he had deliberately selected each word to judge me with, hurling those words at me.

He kept repeating he wanted to live. He went so far as to indicate his desire to work with me after he got home, even noting the political party he wanted to join.

"Karajima's dead, so we don't have to hurry back to Japan," his wife joked while making cloth tags for their luggage.

Her casualness annoyed me.

It was at that moment they received word the returnees would meet at six the next morning and embark in the afternoon. The invalid's eyes brightened, his wife stood up in high spirits. I helped them pack quickly, and after that I purchased enough food for three days. Then I went home to get my own bags ready. On the way I bought the medicine my landlady had asked for. She was cooking when I entered the kitchen. In one hand she held the axe.

"I see. So tomorrow you're finally leaving. Well, congratulations!" she said smiling, the axe in her hand.

I wanted to leave Shanghai as soon as possible. I wanted to separate myself from the streets that had dirtied my hands with Karajima's blood. I didn't think about the fascinating complexity of Shanghai or the monotony of Japan. I wasn't even thinking about what to expect in Japan, about actual possibilities. I even forgot the sick man's feelings, the sentiments of his wife. All I could think of was my own part in Karajima's death. All I could think about was that I had attacked with the axe in my hand, that it had cut deeply into his neck, that I had seen the color of his eyes as he lay dying, had heard his groans at the end.

The next day it continued to rain. The roll call at the meeting place, the loading of baggage onto trucks, the luggage inspection at the depot, the reloading into trucks and unloading at the wharf, the transfer to the ship, the invalids on stretchers carried into sick bay—I had worked to the point of exhaustion.

The hospital ship was a rebuilt training vessel for a merchant marine school. In the evening the embarkation was completed. The student crew and invalids' attendants were covered with sweat and dust. We didn't even have enough energy to laugh. We even had to put the invalids on the floor of the dining salon.

Due to fog, our ship, which had set out, spent a day and night at the mouth of the Yangtze. When we were finally underway, the invalid and his wife were seasick from the high waves. So were most of the passengers. I wasn't, and I carried meals and contacted doctors and washed dishes and chamberpots. Most of the time I spent on deck. If the ship made any progress at all, it was only after a sharp incline of thirty degrees. It seemed as if the gray sea rose high above the deck and receded heavily, a portion of the ship's bottom exposed. The cloudy sky was without rain, and when I looked up, the tall, inclining mast cut across the lead-colored sky. The square, overly large life preserver installed on the mast ropes looked like the frame of an oil painting. Inside that white frame was the sea, an austere gloomy background, alternately appearing and disappearing.

I had no desire to talk to the invalid or his wife. The various emotions I had undergone had exhausted me. For companionship I desired only the spectacle of the enormous, heartless sea. The invalid's wife had wanted to talk to me, but I had somehow managed to avoid her. Behind her dragged the shadow of Karajima, and that shadow threatened me.

Passengers were even lying in the corridors. The serious cases were quiet. The frauds, their illnesses invented to get on board, talked together enthusiastically. The officer in charge walked up and down the narrow sick bay corridor that pitched and rolled. During his all-night vigil he kept giving orders. That made any sort of intricate discussion impossible. But when I awoke in the morning and hurried up the flight of stairs, the invalid's wife looked at me with eyes that seemed to close in on me. When she smiled and touched up her hair, she gave me a meaningful look. Given the chance, she'd have grabbed me by the shoulder.

After lunch the third day out, the wind toying with

蝮
の
す
ゑ

her hair and the sun streaming down, she said to me, "Last night my husband mentioned something odd." Since the ship was on an incline, she was bracing her trousered legs, her transparent, white fingers twisted around some rigging.

"He said he's jealous of you. He's come to feel afraid of you. In spite of the gratitude he feels, he says it's unbearable to put up with the idea you're in love with me. He hasn't made anything out of the fact that I'm really the one in love, but that's all he's been thinking about now since Karajima's death. He's quite serious when he says that even though it amazes him, shames him, he can't get rid of that feeling. I asked him how he could say such things when he's so indebted to you. I told him that was what he really ought to be thinking about. He said he understands that quite well. But he's gradually come to hate you. He can't help it. He had to tell me since he feels guilty about keeping these feelings to himself."

She smiled as if to please me, but then she suddenly became sad and frightened and grabbed my arm.

"You're annoyed, aren't you? Annoyed that I'm just talking nonsense. You've come to dislike me. I'm a bother, aren't I?"

I shook my head as I watched the rising and falling waves.

"I'm just worried."

"Do you still love me?"

"I'm so weighted down I can't think of anything."

"What's worrying you so much?"

The waves struck the side of the ship, the sound muffled. The cold spray fell on my hands and face.

"Karajima? My husband?"

"Everything, everything that concerns my being alive."

The sunlight was pouring down brilliantly, and the

silver-gray crests of the waves glittered. Pitching and rolling, they streamed away. Then the thick walls of salt water crumbled, rolling down hills, splitting into ravines. That huge movement was precise and sharp. But even the immense, clean-cut movement of that brilliant ocean couldn't drown my gloom. I felt, in fact, as if I were standing alone, steeped in a gloom fully exposed to the overflowing brilliant vitality of nature.

I continued to worry about what I had done, something heavy and uncomfortable clogged in my chest.

The ship's doctor had informed me the invalid wouldn't survive the trip. Undoubtedly the invalid himself knew. I too had seen the omen in the color of his weak eyes, in the movement of his throat when he drank water. Obviously he was afraid of me. Even if he wasn't, he'd get nervous and irritable each time I touched him. Without her having told me about it, I had easily guessed his change in attitude. I had neither hoped for his death nor waited for it. It had been settled he'd die. There was no need to hope or wait. I nursed him faithfully and calmly. His wife and I watched over him. In time he would just die. How agonizing it must have been for him to know the obvious. No longer did it matter to him that something had existed between his wife and Karajima, that Karajima had been murdered, that he thought I was the murderer, or even that the ship was continually getting closer to Japan. What must have been weighing on his mind second by second was that his wife and I watched over him while death was closing in on him, that we would stay alive, not die with him.

Once he had asked in a barely audible whisper, "When he died, you were looking at him, weren't you?"

As he spoke he was facing the wall in a corner of the room, but I was startled and stared at him. He hadn't intended to make anyone hear him, nor could his voice actually be heard. Yet in that feeble, hoarse whisper that

蝮
の
す
ゑ

had started talking about Karajima's death, I had sensed some hidden grudge against me. And yet, his words might have been explained as coming from a fever and exhaustion between sleep and waking.

"Seeing him die, did you understand what was on his mind? You see, I do. Completely understand. I understand . . . what . . . he was thinking . . . as about to die." I had felt as if the invalid's pathetically sunken eyes were faintly shining under his thin eyebrows.

"How strange . . . that as I'm dying, you're calmly alive. That's what he was thinking." The sick man tried to move his neck, probably to raise his head, but he couldn't.

"That's what I'm thinking now." Then he was silent. Contemptuously he shut his eyes as if he had achieved some great feat. He had made the last assertion of his life. At least he had made his point. His haggard features stubbornly and coldly indicated he had. His unrelenting maliciousness and uncompromising hostility oozed out over the entire surface of his discolored skin.

She had said he started hating me. That hadn't surprised me. What had been crushing me was his conviction that his thoughts and Karajima's were identical at the point of death. It was no surprise that he had guessed Karajima's mental state during those final moments. It was natural for the invalid to have said to me, "How strange that as I'm dying, you're calmly alive." Yet I couldn't believe that Karajima, who had suddenly been killed, and the invalid, slowly dying of illness, could reach the same thought, especially that the thought of two men who had been enemies should coincide. Obviously though, the invalid was drawing closer to Karajima and joining his camp of the dead. That, apparently, was the invalid's way of threatening us.

By the time we entered Kagoshima Bay, the waves had not yet quieted down. The ashes of Sakurajima trailed in the sky and made the streets of Kagoshima white and dim. We hadn't come across a single Japanese vessel until we entered the harbor. The sea without ships, the town covered with volcanic ash, everything looked dreary and spent. But the repatriates were quite thrilled. A farewell party with entertainment was going on. Halfway through the singing of "Oh! Who Thinks Not of Homeland!" I went out on deck. As I expected, the invalid's wife followed me, moving next to me, looking out at the sea at night.

"We've finally come home together," she said.

The chilly night had subdued her, or perhaps her relief on reaching Japan had. She was quite resigned. For her that was unprecedented.

"What do you intend to do? Separate at once, go away somewhere?"

"I've no place in particular to go," I said.

"It's all right if you want to break up." She smiled awkwardly. "But I've something I want to tell you and get it over with. I know who killed Karajima. I've been wanting to tell you."

She spoke quietly, gently. Her pale profile with its graceful curve didn't seem the least self-conscious. It seemed innocent and fresh.

"I asked someone to. Not a Japanese. A person you hire for murder. A person I knew. I couldn't help worrying about you. I didn't know whether or not I hated Karajima that much to kill him at the last moment. But I wanted to murder anybody likely to kill you. I couldn't help it. Even now I feel it was better to have had him murdered. Even though I instigated it, I don't regret it in the least. I'm not suffering for it. So you don't have to worry about him. You had no connection with it from the very first. I was the one that got you mixed up in it. The responsibility is only Karajima's and mine and my husband's. So there's no need for you to suffer. I'd never

蝮
の
す
ゑ

87

have done it if you were to suffer the least bit for it. I can only think of how sorry I am to have caused you any trouble. When you copied your documents and drank sake, you were quite happy. You were confident. You looked so different from us. I knew that when I came to you. How much better if I had ended only as your customer. Forgive me for involving you in our difficulties. But I was really fond of you. That at least is the truth. I'm a hopeless case I think. But I've never felt like tormenting anyone. I've never felt like doing that, not even to my husband, not even to Karajima. But before I knew it, I was tormenting them. I couldn't stand it if I've gone that far as to torment you. Since you came on board, I've been unhappy about your attitude, but I've thought and thought about it, and I've come to reconcile myself to the fact that I'm to blame. So you really can believe you've absolutely nothing to do with us. Absolutely nothing. I loved you, and that's all there was to it."

She wasn't even slightly agitated. Nor was she hysterical. She spoke quite sympathetically, as a beautiful nurse does in washing a wound with pure water. I hadn't expected that. It increased my feeling of tenderness for her.

"Still, you did go out to attack Karajima for me that night."

"I had to."

"Once you said you couldn't stake your life on anything, but it wasn't true after all, was it? In fact, you're probably the type that's anxious to throw his life away."

"Perhaps."

"Don't, please!"

Her face changed, as if she could no longer bear the strain.

"Live. Don't die. Please, please."

A chorus of voices rose from the deck below: *That's the mountain I knew when I was a child; that's the river.* The children and old men were singing in chorus. At times the wind made their voices weak, at times strong.

We heard someone running up the steps. The doctor in his white operating gown appeared on deck. He called out her name. He turned around and noticed us, and he came up, his slippers dragging. In a slow yet tense voice he told her the invalid had taken a turn for the worse.

蝮
の
す
ゑ

LUMINOUS MOSS

IN THE MIDDLE of September, when the sight of the last red petals of the sweetbriar and its bright, red, full-grown berries can be enjoyed at their best, I traveled to Rausu in Hokkaido. I had chosen the right moment for my trip since I hadn't yet seen these flowers and berries.

The thorns and leaves of the sweetbriar make you think of the rose. The leaves, sturdy enough to survive in the desert sands of the windswept north, are dark green; and the berries, which gently yet in a dignified sort of way dot the hedge formed by the leaves along the bus route, are a radish red. Shaped like crushed balls, the berries resemble crimson-lacquered wood carvings.

As you board the bus in front of Nemuro-Shibetsu Station, the bus that goes to Port Rausu, you can see the Straits of Nemuro on your right. You can't help but notice Kunajiri Island lying flat on the blue surface of the sea.

Actually, the island could have been observed from your train after it passed through the vast wilderness and approached its final destination at Nemuro-Shibetsu. But before you had time to think about the fact that you had been looking at one of the Kuril Islands—now owned by the Soviet Union—or that you were at the "border," you were on your bus heading up and down the hills of the white, dry road along a beach that was continually offering you a view of that "foreign land" just seventeen miles away at its nearest point.

Though I have called it a "foreign land," it is only an ordinary island. It has green hills, and the furrows along its blue mountains can easily be made out in the distance.

ひかりごけ

93

Quite obviously you are at the "border," but it is only a quiet beach without soldiers or bunkers or barbed wire to create any tension. All you see are grazing horses, sometimes running along the sand toward the waves, and crows resting on stakes. Whenever you come across a stream winding into the sea, you also discover a fishing village. The "border" is a lonely, isolated spot, though they say a good year of fishing in the district produces Hokkaido's fifth or sixth highest taxpayer.

No matter how often I tried to convince myself that the island beyond was foreign territory or that I was at the "border," I always ended up losing the inexplicable feeling of irritation readers of Tokyo newspapers are left with as they scan the nerve-racking and exaggerated articles about this area.

The calm water of the straits is steeped in a dark blue that reminds you of the sea at Izu. The innumerable leaves on the cliffs reflect the bright sunshine. Close to the left Mt. Rausu rises sharply. To keep out the winter winds that blow down from above, the fishing villagers set up long logs high against the outside walls of their homes that stand facing the mountain—this in spite of the fact that their side of the peninsula, the coastal area along the straits, has a much gentler landscape than the other side looking out on the Sea of Okhtosk. Certainly at this time of the year you can enjoy the sight of the beautiful flowers and berries of the sweetbriar in weather which is mild and bright, but you have to remember that this particular clemency is quite short—decidedly exceptional for the area. We ought to keep these facts in mind before we proceed with an unusual incident that occurred in the middle of a severe winter. The inhabitants of cities are quite likely to overlook the importance of landscape and climate in determining events.

Rausu derives from an Ainu word. It was given that name because long ago the Ainu killed bear and deer in the area and left the entrails and bones scattered around. It is safe to assume, therefore, that before the incursion of the Japanese, the aboriginal Ainu not only had fish but plenty of meat to devour to their hearts' content.

A truck piled high with crabs passed our bus along a narrow road in a ravine. Another truck loaded with lumber roared by. I saw houses under construction in some of the prosperous villages that had had a heavy catch. Rumbling down a steep slope, our bus crossed a small shallow river meandering along the ravine, and we drove through a dreary-looking village. Once again the bus slowly made its way up a steep incline, and when we reached Rausu, it was just beginning to grow dark. Though the salmon season was hardly underway and there had not yet been any real catch to foretell a good year of fishing, a boy from some village was carrying a bulging salmon as he boarded the bus.

On the mountain side of the main street of Rausu were a temple, a primary school and a junior high, a fishermen's co-operative, a village office, and a drugstore. On the seashore side were five or six inns—nearly ten if you include those under construction, their mud walls still unfinished. I felt there were too many inns for a place this deserted. I picked out an old mediocre one-storied inn. Just about dusk, when the brilliance of red charcoal in an open pit steadily deepens, I was being led into the main room.

As I looked out at the blue darkness and watched the daylight diminish, I was waiting for the electricity to be turned on. I asked about it when a middle-aged woman came in to serve some tea. "There's a movie in the village tonight," she said. She seemed to suggest the electricians were extorting money by deliberately disrupting the service on a special occasion of this sort. I went outside and walked along the many stones in the garden. Instead of a hedge at the end of the path there were rows of firewood piled on top of one another. Directly beyond was the sea. The sharp brilliance of the evening sun pierced through the dark blue expanding curtain of night. The black clouds almost completely hid Kunajiri Island, a portion of which flashed in jagged outline under the sun's rays. Along the beach, beyond the area for refuse, four or five fishing boats had been pulled up at a sharp angle. There were black crows perching motionlessly on them. As usual at this hour, the sea was rising. The evening wind was cold. The straits, whose only aim seemed to be to turn into a vast area of black, appeared so impressively solid and powerful that the boats exposed on the beach looked fragile, their position precarious, as if they had been made out of gray paper. What I saw before me was not so much a "border," first of all, as the northern sea on a September night, that immense body of water and wind which, by turning into a black shape, had overcome by sheer power innumerable tensions and had enveloped them silently.

In the room next to mine were a botany teacher and his pupil. Long after I had returned to my room, they had remained standing in the garden to watch the waves at night.

We had fine autumn weather again the next day. The morning sun and the charcoal fire made the village office too hot. I had wanted to meet the mayor, who owned a large collection of Ainu relics, but unfortunately he was out. The assistant mayor kept on talking enthusiastically about the village, about practical, down-to-earth matters.

Later, as I went to see the luminous moss with the junior high school principal, he told me a good deal more about life in the village.

The principal, probably in his thirties, was tall and thin. Because of the gentle and bashful smile always on his face, he didn't look like the type that can stand up against the adversities of nature and man. A scraggly beard against his yellowish skin, trousers thin and faded, coarse canvas shoes. No doubt he had seen through his role and destiny as an obscure little principal in a fishing village on the border. He had apparently resigned himself to playing out the game, somewhat humorously with a hesitating yet amiable smile. He was a gentle person who had no intention of putting you on the defensive or opposing you. Unlike the reckless bus driver or the pragmatic assistant mayor, the principal seemed to have been deliberately overlooked when the violent energies of nature had been handed out.

"I haven't seen the luminous moss either," the principal said.

Seemingly without vigor in his walk as he went on ahead of me, he made his lean body waver somewhat as if he were floating—perhaps that was because of the light weight of his canvas shoes.

Rausu is the last stop on the bus route, and you can go no further except by small boat. Still, the road the bus takes continues all the way to the end of the village. The side of the road bordering on the sea has a stone embankment, the surface of the water shining phosphorescently, almost gorgeously, against it. A complex of colors as various as those in seaweed and rock moss is reflected, the water near the shore changing from one color to another—purple, black, brown, gray, blue—as the waves move the strands of seaweed to and fro.

Even the engine of a fishing boat heading smoothly toward the Soviet border sounded carefree.

We came upon a husky fisherman and his wife weighing bundles of dried seaweed in front of a warehouse. They handled the bundles as if they were precious. The seaweed, neatly tied with straw rope, had been shaped into perfect squares.

As we walked along, several people noticed us, and

ひ
か
り
ご
け

one of them bowed to the principal. He returned the greeting by nodding slightly, with a sort of bashful smile. He seemed so faltering in these actions, so uncertain of himself, that the fishermen, by contrast, appeared all the more impressive with their solid shoulders, the steady look in their eyes.

"Oh? You haven't seen the luminous moss?" I asked him.

I wondered why. Living here and being the principal as well, why had he never taken his pupils to see it?

At Makkaushi (which means "an abundant place for butterburs") the shore is sandwiched between a cliff and a huge rock in the sea. The entrance to the cave opening toward the sea looks like the enormous mouth of a whale. As I went in deeper, I looked back and saw the horizon coming up to the center of the semicircle formed by the rock. It's probably better to call the cave a hole in the side of a mountain, a hole that narrows increasingly the deeper in you go. The rock ceiling became lower as we climbed a slope of red earth, but even at the very end of the cave it was still not completely dark.

"We ought to find some moss in here," the principal said, looking around. "But I'm not sure where."

In spite of the fact that the end of the cave was so low we had to bend, the rest of its interior was fairly high and wide. In the middle of the cave, I found buried in the ground a large flat rock that would have been ideal for a garden stone. The walls of rock and the earth were wet with drops of water falling from above. The green moss we found on the walls and ground, however, wasn't luminous. As I reached out to touch it, I discovered it felt the same as any ordinary kind of moss.

We had to stoop somewhat as we walked back and forth a while. Since the cave's interior had no intricate turns or notches and was, in fact, a simple semicircle that could be seen to its very end at a glance, the luminous moss ought certainly to have been in view. But neither of us could find any.

"Located some yet?" he asked apologetically.

"No. I've no idea where it is," I said.

The various postures, positions, and lines of vision I had tried hadn't helped us at all. Finally I merely stood there without hope of ever finding any of the stuff. Then, as I happened to vacantly glance around, I saw, at the very spot I had haphazardly looked at, a pinpoint of inexplicably beautiful golden green glowing on no other than the moss I had already become tired of watching.

"There it is!" I said. "There!"

"Where?" asked the principal.

"A little to your right. Look!"

I stood out of the way while the principal was stumbling around, and from another direction this time, I saw the golden green moss with its quiet glow. In fact, the first glow of moss I had seen had already turned an ordinary green.

"Yes—there's some more at your feet. Yes, it's certainly glowing," the principal said. The discovery made him sound somewhat happy, though he hadn't bothered to raise his voice much.

When someone else pointed to it, you couldn't find the moss glowing, but if you looked about casually, you might discover a pinpoint of light, like the color of some precious rug, suddenly appear from one of the golden green sparks. So faint was the light, you were moved by the realization that light could be so small, so reserved, so crystal sharp. Instead of describing the glow of the moss as golden green, it would be more accurate to say that somehow the golden green moss was transformed into light itself. The light was not shining on the moss. It was steeping itself into the very essence of the moss. I felt as if the moss were trying to absorb the light into itself rather than to shed it.

ひ
か
り
ご
け

99

As I looked back, I detected the moss I had been stomping on without even realizing it was also glowing, revealing faint traces of the black footprints left by my shoes.

"So it's all over the place," I said. "We've been stepping on National Treasures!"

I could feel the quiet vitality of the moss I had trampled on filling the entire cave gradually. If I uttered a sound, I felt the walls and ceiling of the cave would reverberate with the coarse, wild voices of carnivorous animals. The moss had dignity as it glowed, but when it didn't, it looked like the torn or nappy part of a rug, a straw mat, a blanket, or any other commonplace thing of that order. And the way the moss grew on the rocks made it seem much weaker than those threadbare articles. Nothing in the moss itself suggested that ferocious tenacity which makes this veteran of all plants survive for so many years. In fact, in this place which every living thing had abandoned, the moss had kept out of the way of all other things, kept itself aloof as a thin surface layer. Its entire appearance failed to oppress me with that sinister threat so peculiar to the moss family as it contrives its odd little tricks in the battle for existence.

No matter how good my vision might have been or how adept I might have become in the art of observation, it was hardly to be expected that the glow from the moss would flood the cave and transform it into a flowery garden of light. The moment a faint fraction of the brocade of light was visible at one spot, it shifted to another, and, in addition, that lonely glow, without increasing or becoming more intense, remained a single color of golden green.

We went down the gravel road from the cave and in the energetic and brilliant sunshine along the shore walked back to the village.

"The papers say there's been a lot of trouble at the

border, but now that I'm right on the spot, it seems awfully quiet," I said.

"Yes, it is," said the principal.

"The Russians aren't even turning the searchlights on, are they? I was watching the sea last night."

"No, they're not. But they will soon," the principal said in an unconcerned way. "They use them when we send out our squid boats. The sea looks like it's on fire when many of our boats are out. From the distance it's as if a large city has suddenly come into being. The Russians put the lights on to see what we're up to."

No one was on the pier. A long white streak left by a fishing boat in the far distance was seen across the blue surface of the water.

I had heard that after the long winter hibernation the people of Rausu say spring comes riding in by bus.

"It's quite a relief to have the first bus in," the principal said.

"When's that?" I asked.

"About the tenth of May. It's hard on us till then. For one thing, we're short of cigarettes. The price gets higher and higher. What was that you said? The mail? It's the only thing brought in by horse-drawn sleds during winter. Oh yes, it happened on that trip of mine last winter. I'd gone out to bring back some test questions. I had quite an ordeal when our boat drifted off course."

The Ministry of Education had given a simultaneous, country-wide examination, so the principal's school could not have postponed it. Consequently, he had gone by fishing boat to Shibetsu in February to get the forms. He had arrived safely, but on the return, a violent wind had suddenly headed his boat toward the Kuril Islands. The ice-drifts all over the straits kept his boat from making any progress. In addition, the wind was blowing toward Russian territory and brought his boat close to Kunajiri Island, far beyond the border. The ice-drifts on the

ひ
か
り
ご
け

101

straits are not huge blocks like icebergs but small splinters. Yet when they close in on one another, the principal said, they are powerful enough to block a ship's course. He had climbed the roof of the engine room and had looked for an opening in the white expanse of the field of ice.

"Weren't you worried about what they might have done to you if you had drifted onto Russian territory and been caught?" I asked.

"No, not about that in particular," he said. "I'd have been in real trouble if I hadn't returned with the examinations, so I had to get back at any cost. You talk of Russian territory, but there's not a man or a sign of anything in sight. They say piles of squid are heaped up on the beach over there."

Without a trace of exaggeration or forced enthusiasm, he apparently was enjoying the memory of his ordeal. He had shouted out directions from the roof of the cabin as the pilot steered the boat on its zigzag course. The usual two-hour trip to Rausu had taken them three days.

He also talked about climbing Mt. Rausu. From Rausu there is no good route up the mountain, though one exists on the other side. He had scaled the mountain through the shortest, most reasonable path by tracing the footprints and excrement of bears (that is, with the help of the wisdom of bears). After hearing these adventures on land and sea, I concluded that this gangling, delicate-looking man had some hidden endurance, some power that might be called "nonresistant resistance."

What the principal most enjoyed talking about was a horrifying incident that had taken place at Pekin Promontory.

"The Captain came to Rausu good and plump after he had eaten some of his crew. Fantastic people really do exist!" The principal burst out laughing as if he thought the story was so funny he couldn't restrain himself.

"Since the Captain didn't say a word about it, nobody knew at first. It turned out he hadn't eaten only one person as we thought, but two or three. A really fantastic character!"

The principal's laughingly spoken "really fantastic character!" was as innocent and pleasant as his lightly poking fun at a boardinghouse friend who had made a blunder. On that road along the coast in the fine autumn weather, his voice sounded so carefree that the disturbing note of "eating human flesh" didn't seem particularly sickening.

While walking through the scenery I have been describing, I was so fascinated by this "incident of eating human flesh" that I could almost feel the "creases of my mind" actually contract with a snap. And even while answering the principal with "Is that so?" and "It was during the last part of the war then?" I was conscious that the subject was turning from second to second into small black pellets in the depths of the "Makkaushi Cave" of my mind, beginning to function furiously and to rave, urging and imploring for the earliest possible release.

Suddenly recalling the dark and melancholy look of anger and grief on the face of the Ainu linguist Mori, I felt he would have been delighted to hear about this incident.

I had reached Sapporo on August 25th. That turned out to be the last day of the Conference for the Study of Northern Peoples in Japan, especially the Ainu. It had been an unusual meeting since experts from many fields, ethnologists, medical scholars, biologists, and linguists, all the way to students of local history, had participated in the debates. The first thing I did on my arrival was get in touch with Mori, and he came right over to my inn. I had known him quite well when I had lived in Sapporo, and I had found his scholarly pursuits and his

ひ
か
り
ご
け

103

future of special interest. The moment he had entered my room, he began to attack the Conference with a bombardment of sarcasm. "It's brilliantly exposed the enormous stupidity of Japanese scholars on the Ainu!" he began. The weary smile on his face which was dark and pale from illness, the long eyelashes in the sunken cavities of his large eyes, the thin cheeks that made his cheekbones look noticeably high—all these seemed aflame with the sulfuric fires of his rancor and defiance.

What had particularly enraged him was an item in a report at one of the meetings. A scholar had made the comment that an ancient Ainu tribe had once practiced cannibalism. Of course the reference had almost nothing to do with the main theme of the paper, but the scholar had offered the statement rather carelessly to supplement a point in his talk. Mori had instantly sprung forward with the ferocious intensity of a tiger, demanding what sources and legends the lecturer had as evidence. Since the subject was quite out of place at a conference where many scholars of Ainu extraction were present, the moderator was anxious to appease Mori with an apology, so the situation had been patched up for the time being.

From my experience with Japanese authorities on the Ainu, I have found all of them humanitarians, serious-minded persons whose love of Ainu culture makes them anxious to keep it from perishing and gives them much more sympathy and understanding for the Ainu than the average Japanese has. Quite obviously the man that had committed the blunder hadn't meant to be unkind. Mori himself had been on the most friendly terms with his fellow-scholars. Yet even while recognizing these facts, Mori couldn't restrain himself, couldn't help starting a wild uproar in the presence of his learned colleagues.

As I had looked at Mori at that time, I remember not being able to understand why a report that a member of a certain tribe (or several or even scores of members) had once eaten human flesh should have so upset him. What had struck home to me instead was the look of suffocation filled with a mixture of disdain, loneliness, and grief on the face of this highest intellectual of Ainu descent as he said with disgust, "Some of us scholars, you know, have to conceal our Ainu origins." Had Mori only known the details of the horrifying incident at Pekin Promontory, he might have made a frontal counterattack of his own by insisting that a human flesh-eater existed, not only among the Ainu, but among the unmistakably "pure" Japanese, in fact, "among the people under the glorious reign of the Emperor when their war spirit was at high tide!" Mori could then have harangued the Conference that day by advocating the mobilization of all the scholars convened there so that a contemporary Japanese, the Captain himself, not an unknown Ainu veiled in the mist of a distant past, might be put on the rack and questioned from every angle of ethnology, ethics, medicine, psychology, economics, and politics.

After I returned to my inn, I had another pleasant talk for an hour with the principal. But the outline of the incident still remained vague due to his way of referring to it—with his "Fantastic characters really do exist!"—his words were much too elusive. It was only after the principal had introduced me to the young Mr. Sato, who compiled and wrote *The History of Rausu Village,* and I had received a copy from him that I came to know some of the real facts about the event.

Had the writer of the *History* not been young, as Sato was, he would hardly have put that creepy, disastrous incident on the records of his hometown. First of all, the event hadn't occurred in his village, nor was the Captain from Rausu. It didn't make much sense to put the situation on record and give the impression that the village was barbarously uncivilized. Furthermore, there was absolutely nothing murderous or dismal about Rausu.

ひかりごけ

The place is so peaceful, in fact, that with hardly anything worth recording, one is almost tempted to insert a chapter entitled, "An Incident of Cannibalism Involving a Shipwrecked Captain."

"Early in the morning of 3 December 1944, at the apex of the Greater East Asia War, the Akatsuki Squadron, charged with an urgent task, left Port Nemuro for Otaru via Shiretoko Peninsula."

Thus begins the description, like that of a novel, of the great literary effort Mr. Sato had so laboriously worked at.

"Already the morning was proving to be threatening. As the Squadron passed just off the coast of Rausu, heavy winds and snow began. The snowstorm was typical of this region. Despite the immense difficulties of coping with the snow and rough seas, the Squadron (numbering seven to nine ships in all) remained in close formation, its course straight for Shiretoko Point in the discharge of its urgent duties."

The wrecked ship in question was the Fifth Seijin Maru (27 tons) with a crew of six under her Captain. That the *History* refers only to the Captain's age (37) and not his name must have been due to chronicler Sato's kind consideration. Fifty-five kilometers north of Rausu the ship developed engine trouble and was unable to proceed.

The anchor proved useless because of the snowstorm and violent waves, and the ship drifted on and on. Nevertheless, everyone felt land was close by. But the shoreline was so dotted with reefs it was impossible to get to the beach safely. A young seaman, the ablest swimmer among them, tied a rope around his waist and jumped from the ship ("which was fluttering like a leaf") into the freezing, sharp-edged December sea. Despite the fact that the Captain had no doubt ordered the man to act, the name of this brave youth, "abounding in the spirit of sacrifice in accepting this dangerous assignment," is unknown. At any rate, clinging to the rope the youth had brought to shore, the Captain and other crew members followed, roughly tossed about through the waves. The Captain, who was cast ashore unconscious due to fatigue and cold, came to after his buttocks had been continually slapped by the youngest member of the crew, the nineteen-year-old Nishikawa.

On the storm-driven, snow-laden beach, Nishikawa and the Captain saw the other crew members prostrate or hurtled through the waves. They shouted at the men, urging them on. "We'll freeze to death if we stay here! Let's get to the other side over the mountain and find shelter from the storm!" The Captain and Nishikawa started walking hand in hand. The *History* is extremely vague in describing the scene at this stage of the incident. No reference is made as to whether or not the entire crew of seven actually started together or how many of them eventually reached the hut. Perhaps the statements of the Captain were not clear.

Their drenched clothing was frozen as solidly as steel plates. Their hands and legs were as insensible as wooden clubs.

The hut they discovered was an overnight stopping place used by fishermen gathering sea urchins in the spring and seaweed in the summer. The Captain and his men had pushed and waded through the incessantly falling snow, and about evening of the day of shipwreck, they found the hut half-buried in the blizzard. Even after stumbling into the shelter, they would have instantly frozen to death had it not been for a box of matches on the shelf and some good firewood inside.

On February 3, 1945, the Captain turned up at Rushiya, twenty-one kilometers from Rausu. Exactly two months had elapsed since the shipwreck. "Veiled in impenetrable darkness is the kind of life he or they had led

ひかりごけ

inside the hut during those two months." The confessions and secrets of the Captain, as the sole survivor of the tragedy, are subject to any kind of interpretation and speculation.

Of course the Captain, as long as it cast no ill reflections on him, had talked about what had happened on the day of the shipwreck and what he had been through afterwards—that is, how he had abandoned the hut after enduring emaciation to the point of collapse, how overjoyed he had been to find the tracks of a skier in the snow, how anxiously he had waited to be rescued.

The fisherman who had found the Captain immediately reported to the village office. On February 4, the day after his discovery, the Captain was sent to Rausu and given shelter and medical care in a room at an inn. In no time at all there spread throughout the village the "beautiful wartime drama" of a courageous Captain. Overcome with sympathy and admiration, members of the Patriotic Women's Association, youth groups, and primary school children came rushing with gifts, day in and day out, for the hero.

"But all the Captain did was express his deep gratitude. He lay quietly in bed without saying much."

This fine prose description from the pen of Mr. Sato is no doubt a successful portrayal of the suffering and anxiety in the Captain's mind.

After receiving the report from the village office, the headquarters of the Akatsuki Squadron sent an on-the-spot investigation team to Rausu under the command of one of its officers. Of course the purpose of the group was not to investigate a crime but to pick up the bodies of the war dead. That time of the year makes the discovery of corpses quite difficult, so only the body of one Fujimaki (20) could be accounted for. Standing, frozen, leaning against a cliff, it was found buried in snow. A wooden monument was erected at the site. The inscription reads: "Place of death of the military civilian, one Fujimaki, sailor on the Fifth Seijin Maru."

In early May when the fishermen went out to Pekin Promontory to gather sea urchins, the crime came to light. During those approximately ninety days, from the Captain's rescue to that moment, his suffering and anxiety, presumably, had been steadily on the increase. This interval alone would provide enough material for a thick psychological novel.

At first the fishermen came across a floating apple crate jammed in among the ice-drifts off the shore of the promontory. They hoisted it up and found it stuffed with a cranium, hand and leg bones, and human skin. The terror-stricken men reported to the police, who, upon inspection, proved that the bones, though broken into fragments, exactly totaled those of one human being.

The skin, which was still attached to the cranium, had a two-inch growth of hair. The hands had been cut off at the wrists, the legs at the ankles. All the bones had turned pure white except those of the ribs, which were a nauseating rust color. At the bottom of the crate were two patches of skin, one ripped off from the chest to the abdomen, the other from the shoulders to the waist. In addition, they discovered a jacket with the Captain's name on it.

Needless to say, an entire troop of prosecution officials rushed to the scene. The dead body of another seaman, one Yoshida (35), was found on that occasion (though Mr. Sato's *History* fails to specify the location). They had come across Yoshida lying as if he were agreeably asleep, his overcoat on, his face turned seaward, his arms stretched forward.

A summary of the Captain's confession follows:

The only ones that had finally reached the hut were Nishikawa and the Captain. The next morning Nishikawa had picked up a seagull on the beach, and they had

ひ
か
り
ご
け

109

eaten it after boiling it with some bean soup stored in the hut. Unable to alleviate their hunger, the two men often searched for food along the shore. They caught a "tokkari" floating among the ice-drifts, took it to the hut, and ate it as sparingly as possible. (According to Mr. Genzo Sarashina's article in the first volume of *The Study of the Northern Districts*, published by the Hokkaido Folklore Association, the Ainu call seals "tokkari" when they are on land and "chiramantepu" when they are on the sea.) But at the beginning of January, Nishikawa and the Captain ran out of seal meat too. The ice-drifts made it impossible for them to gather seaweed. Nor was it possible to find any dead seagulls and "tokkari." They had encouraged each other with the idea of holding out until the ice-drifts receded in the offing, and for more than a dozen days they had eked out a bare existence on bean soup and hot water. But on the morning of January 16, Nishikawa died of hunger, exhaustion, and cold. Overwhelmed by a complicated feeling, the Captain had cried out aloud while clinging to the dead body.

"I didn't have a single thing to eat," stated the Captain. "When I thought I would eventually end up like Nishikawa, something bestial suddenly rose up inside me, and like a madman and with the same sensations I had in tearing off the skin from the seal, I cut the flesh from Nishikawa's dead body."

By the end of January the human flesh was also gone. The sea was still packed with clashing ice-drifts. As long as the Captain couldn't get hold of any birds, fish, or human bodies, his death was inevitable. Since he would eventually end up a corpse himself, he made the decision to go out and walk as far as possible, and he abandoned the hut. (But in view of the fact that the description of this scene is followed by such words as "broiling the leftover flesh and carrying it with him," it is evident that the captain had started out before completely finishing all the flesh. He was obviously a man of prudent calculation.)

The Captain was convicted of mutilating and abandoning a corpse.

What I found most interesting were Mr. Sato's detective story-like conjectures added to the end of his report.

"Henceforth," he writes, "we may permit ourselves to indulge in dreadful fancies."

The first of his "dreadful fancies" is that both Nishikawa and the Captain had devoured the bodies of the three seamen who couldn't be located after all attempts to find them had failed. If the two men had eaten these three corpses during the forty-four days from the shipwreck to the date of Nishikawa's death (though the Captain was said to have stated at the time of his rescue that Nishikawa was missing), they would have eaten one body every fifteen days. This figure, Mr. Sato indicates, corresponds well with the theoretical calculation of speed of flesh consumption and passage of time. His next conjecture is that the Captain murdered Nishikawa. When no more human flesh remained, Mr. Sato imagined, the two men who had eaten human meat found themselves in the position of killing or being killed so that on January 16, the Captain killed Nishikawa in order to eat him.

To justify these "dreadful fancies," Mr. Sato points out (1) that from a shipwrecked crew of seven, the bodies of three were never found; (2) that after eating Nishikawa's flesh, the Captain took the trouble to put the victim's bones in a crate and set it adrift at sea; (3) that a great many bloodstains were discovered not only on several straw mats Nishikawa is said to have slept on but through the flooring beneath those mats.

It's unfortunate that I'm unable to introduce the prosecution's indictment because the complete record was not attached to Mr. Sato's *History*. But supposing that the sentence had been imposed before August 15, 1945, that is, before the end of the war in which killing the

ひ
か
り
ご
け

enemy was the one and only desire of our nation, I wonder if the punishment would not have been lighter than had it been given after the war when "democracy" is everybody's motto. Had the victims been Americans or British, on the other hand—American or English "white beasts" as they were customarily referred to—the "human flesh-eater" might have been found not guilty.

The ten minutes I had talked with Mr. Sato around the open-pit fire in the drugstore where he lived with his parents was hardly enough time for me to discuss the incident. Later the principal and Mr. Sato came to see me off. They stood by the window of my bus and then continued to wave quietly for a long while after it had started.

As my bus drew near Shibetsu, a white cloud that reminded me of Kunajiri Island appeared in the intensely blue sky over the eastern sea. The base of the cloud was as straight as the horizon at sea, and the upper contours of the cloud were exactly like those of Kunajiri, so I felt as if the flatly extended form of the island had been cut out of white paper. The distance from which I was looking at the cloud gave me the impression that the real island and the white cloud in the sky were the same size.

Two months have already passed since the end of my thirty-three-day trip to Hokkaido, and I am still trying to figure out the best way to turn this incident into a novel. At the very least the event contains something quite nauseating, something different in meaning from Sartre's brand of nausea. How dismal the symbol I have in mind, the brilliantly colorful sign of danger, the depressing contrabass range of sound!

Miss Yaeko Nogami sharply delineates in her book *The Kaijin Maru* a murderous drama enacted by seamen threatened with immediate death through starvation. A sailor in her story kills another in order to eat his flesh, but finally fails to, for the captain of *The Kaijin Maru,* unlike his counterpart in the Pekin Promontory episode, was ethically in control of the other men and prohibited cannibalism. Apparently "salvation" in Miss Nogami's novel lies in the fact that even though the crime of murder was committed, the crime of cannibalism was not.

Shohei Ooka's *Fires on the Plain* also has someone starving, the soldier-hero of the novel who reaches the point of putting a piece of human flesh into his mouth (that of a Japanese soldier given him by a companion) but who ends by not swallowing it. Despite the fact that the man is quite capable of meaninglessly shooting a native woman to death, he is discovered excusing himself from an ethical standpoint as he says, "I did kill, but I didn't eat."

By correlating the Pekin Promontory incident, *The Kaijin Maru,* and *Fires on the Plain,* and by following the laws of deduction, we can see what crimes may be committed by men at the extreme limit of hunger without any possible means of escape from that condition: (1) simple murder (2) murder for the purpose of eating human flesh (3) murder for the purpose of cannibalism but not eating (4) murder for the purpose of cannibalism and eating (5) eating the flesh of men who have died from natural causes.

The crime of (2) seems more serious than (1), (4) more serious than (3). But when it comes to the question of determining the greater seriousness of (1) or (5), the problem is so appalling that the comparison itself seems absurd.

To kill human beings; to eat human flesh. The only discernible phenomenon that comes to us through the senses in relation to these two acts is that each exudes a somewhat different odor.

When we focus our most strenuous thought on why the odors are different, we find the answer quite simple: Murders today are so commonplace that they are easily

ひ
か
り
ご
け

113

within view in our twentieth century, whereas cannibalism has almost completely disappeared from the earth. The mass murder in Korea is a recent example of the former crime. And not only there, for we have become habituated to the possibility that the same crime of murder will occur on a tremendous scale somewhere on earth. That premonition may terrify us, but it fails to nauseate us. And although we have a great deal of antipathy toward it, we do not regard the possibility as curious or grotesque.

When, on the other hand, we come to the question of cannibalism, we feel such disgust, no matter what the circumstances, that we literally shudder. We believe the action is uncivilized, barbarous, violent, and profane, and we tell ourselves that the act has nothing to do with us, that it is quite beyond our imagination. It is almost as if we have made up our minds in advance that murder, though much more prevalent, is aristocratic, whereas cannibalism, though in a category all its own, is plebian.

"Civilized men" can commit murder, but they cannot eat human flesh without bringing disgrace on themselves. "Our nation, our race, may murder," they insist, "but we can never commit cannibalism." They are smug in their conviction of the excellence of their nation, an advanced race, one worthy of the blessings of God. A perfect illustration of this smug complacency occurs when the hero of *Fires on the Plain* assures himself he is civilized by reflecting that "I did kill, but I didn't eat."

As a proud manifestation of the power of civilization, weapons of war and their mass production are openly displayed in the newsreels. Cooking utensils for human flesh, on the contrary, are no longer seen in the flatware sections of department stores or in the special exhibit rooms of museums. Of these two types of criminal tools, one has successfully won popular support and is being improved from moment to moment, whereas the other is about to be erased from memory as a secret weapon whose recollection sends a shudder of horror through the human heart. Even public opinion polls on these two crimes reveal an ever-increasing popularity for the one, a rapid decline for the other. All due to the simple reason that the election posters and propaganda cars and platforms of the advocates of murder have reached into the corners of every street, while candidates for cannibalism have been incarcerated long before election day.

I had, at any rate, to give some sort of literary expression to the Pekin Promontory incident, a subject which "civilized" ladies and gentlemen must judge as bizarre and cruel and which they are quite unlikely to welcome as readers. I finally resorted to the strategy of setting the event down as a play. I thought the form of a "closet drama" would best allow the reader's everyday feelings to enter into and merge with the situation through innumerable channels in a not-too-vivid representation, that is, without restricting him to the narrow confines of realism. My only wish is that the reader of this impossible-to-be staged play imagines himself its producer in his own style as he reads. . .

ACT ONE

CHARACTERS
    Captain *(the most sinister-looking man the reader can imagine)*
    Nishikawa, a seaman *(a handsome young man)*
    Hachizo, a seaman
    Gosuke, a seaman

SCENE
    The Makkaushi Cave. About the end of 1944. A severe winter. The last winter of the Pacific war.

ひかりごけ

LUMINOUS MOSS

The reader (that is, the producer) is free to choose any style of performance he wishes, from among the tear-jerking melo-drama, the pathetic recital, the sophisticated comedy for intel-lectuals, and the visionary religious play.

The curtain rises as the rumbling of a snowstorm is heard. The scene is inside the rock-cave. Four men, illumined by the flames of a fire, are squatting silently.

HACHIZO: We the only ones? Only our ship that's run into this kinda bad luck?

[Silence]

No matter what's happened, it can't only be us, can it? Outa ten ships, how come we're the only ones that's got shipwrecked?

[Silence]

If we're the only ones with bad luck, it's a helluva thing to do t'us. Right? All the others gettin' through safe, an' just us in this goddam . . .

GOSUKE: Why not ask Captain?

HACHIZO: It might only just be us. Well sure, it's just us. An' if that's so, we're in for it.

GOSUKE: Even if we ain't the only ones, we're still in for it.

HACHIZO: Yeah. Even if we ain't, we're sure in for it.

GOSUKE: Either way, we're still hungry, ain't we?

HACHIZO: Yeah. Either way we're hungry—that's for sure.

GOSUKE *[derisively]*: Hey, Nishikawa! Nishikawa, say, ya sure workin' hard over there.

[Nishikawa keeps silent, scraping the bone of a seal.]

Well, go right ahead with yer work an' make ya a har-poon an' let's eat a whale!

HACHIZO: Real smart idea he got there, makin' a har-poon outa a seal bone. But what the hell's he gonna catch with it? Huh? Bet no seal or fish are comin' to that beach. There ain't even a single scrap a seaweed out there. I ain't been doin' nothin', but I'm still dizzy 'cause I'm hungry. How come he's goin' to all that trouble over that fancy work that won't come to a damn thing?

GOSUKE: Well, let's leave the kid alone, Hachizo. It don't matter what we do 'cause there ain't no hope a ever gettin' rescued.

HACHIZO: No—that's right. They decided a long time ago a man's gotta die when he don't get nothin' t'eat. It don't matter how ya look at it, we're in for some trouble.

GOSUKE: Just thinkin' a that old, worn-out ship a ours! From the first we knew she wouldn't hold up.

NISHIKAWA: Stop talking about that!

HACHIZO: What's that?

NISHIKAWA: What's the good of complaining? Look at the Captain. He doesn't complain at all. Aren't you forgetting your duty to the Squadron?

HACHIZO: Huh?

NISHIKAWA: We're military civilians, aren't we? Even if we're in a tough spot like this.

HACHIZO: That's right. Military civilians.

NISHIKAWA: If you're military civilians, why can't you act like real soldiers? How can we carry out our sacred war if we don't act like that?

GOSUKE: Hey, Nishikawa! Ya sound mighty good. But look, yer about fallin' on your ass, ain't ya?

HACHIZO: I'll *carry out* our *sacred war* too, I promise ya. If I can *carry it out,* I will, whenever I can. I never hated *carryin' out* things.

GOSUKE: Sure. Nishikawa probably thinks he's Commander a the Squadron. But look, Nishikawa, just ya bring in the Commander right here. What the hell could he do when he's brought in here? Well, bring

ひ
か
り
ご
け

117

in a Colonel! Bring in a General! What could they do in such a stinkin' hole?

NISHIKAWA: We're not the Commander's military civilians! We're military civilians of the Emperor. Of the Emperor! You better remember that.

GOSUKE: Awright, awright. I ain't scared a whoever ya name. What's so special about the Emperor? Ya gonna tell me the Emperor don't feel hungry when he's hungry? Why not just bring the Emperor right here to this goddam hole then?

HACHIZO: Oh, Gosuke, cut it out. It's terrible t'say things like that. Anyway, what's the good a us havin' the Emperor right here?

GOSUKE: He better damn well come here! Bring him in! Let him stay here ten or twenty days chewin' on seal bones!

NISHIKAWA: The hell with you!

[About to jump at Gosuke. The Captain restrains him. The sound of the snowstorm is heard more loudly. Some snowflakes are seen blowing into the cave. All the men come nearer the fire in a close-packed circle.]

HACHIZO: I don't think me or Gosuke done nothin' wrong t'make Nishikawa mad. We just been talkin' about gettin' hungry when there ain't no food.

GOSUKE: That's what got him mad at us.

HACHIZO: Then how the hell should we talk about it?

GOSUKE: We better talk about not bein' hungry or not dyin' even though we got nothin' t'eat.

HACHIZO: I don't like tellin' lies. I don't feel good tellin' lies. Well, then, what'll we talk about? Oh yeah! I heard the Emperor ate seal meat. Get that! I wonder when? I read it in the newspaper.

GOSUKE: Ya sure?

HACHIZO: Didn't ya know? Didn't ya read the menu in the paper for the New Year ceremony at the Imperial Palace? The Steak of the Meat of a Seal from Hokkaido. An' a Raw Coconut from the South Pacific. Eatin' such stuff, the paper said, the Emperor thought about the pains a the soldiers fightin' at the front.

GOSUKE: That so?

HACHIZO: Seal meat's wonderful, no matter who eats it. Boiled or broiled, it's delicious! Ever eat a Ainu dish called *fuibe?* Know how they make it? Ya chop up a seal's guts—bowels, lungs, liver, all that—into real small pieces. Dump in the moustache an' brains too. Ya scramble'm up an' add some sea water for seasonin'. Oh the taste! Nothin's more delicious'n that!

GOSUKE: Yeah?
[Falls down on his side, no longer able to bear the pains in his stomach.]

HACHIZO: What is it, Gosuke? What's wrong? Ya got a stomach-ache? Pull yerself together.
[He stands up and looks after Gosuke.]

NISHIKAWA *[rises and goes beside Gosuke]:* What's the matter with you, Gosuke? Are the pains bad?
[Only the Captain keeps silent, not budging an inch.]

HACHIZO: Gosuke, please, ya ain't gonna die, are ya? Ya ain't!

NISHIKAWA: He looks real funny. He's spouting bubbles like a crab. Captain, is he all right?

CAPTAIN *[standing alone, apart from Gosuke]:* Be helluva while before he dies.

GOSUKE *[barely sitting up, holding his stomach with his hands]:* Captain, I ain't gonna die yet?

CAPTAIN: Just what I been sayin'. Ya ain't dyin' yet.

GOSUKE: When then?

CAPTAIN: I can't tell when, but it ain't today.

GOSUKE: If not today, will I die tomorrow?

NISHIKAWA: Gosuke, we're all going to die. I know you're suffering, but try to bear it, please!

HACHIZO: Yeah. Nishikawa's right. It ain't only Gosuke's gonna die.

ひ
か
り
ご
け

119

GOSUKE: I don't wanna die.

NISHIKAWA: I know you don't. If we die in this lousy hole, it's a dog's death. We still have our duty to perform, you know, don't we? We can't afford to die until we die gloriously in the war.

GOSUKE: I don't wanna die that way neither!

HACHIZO: Take it easy. We can't even die a war death in a stinkin' hole like this. In the first place, there ain't no goddam enemy.

GOSUKE: I don't wanna die at all.

HACHIZO: If ya don't, ya don't have to.

GOSUKE: We'll die separately. We'll each drop off one at a time.

HACHIZO: Well, maybe so.

GOSUKE: Then who's gonna die first?

[Silence]

Oh, yer all keepin' quiet? Ya don't have t'say it 'cause ya know! I'm first!

[Nishikawa and Hachizo avert their faces from the shouting Gosuke. Only the Captain looks straight at Gosuke.]

I—I don't wanna die first!

[Falls down again unable to endure his pain.]

Why don't I wanna die first?—know why? Ya wanna know why?

CAPTAIN *[in a commanding tone]*: Shut up, Gosuke! Shut up and get the hell asleep! Nishikawa, let's get down to the beach and see if we can find anythin'! There might be somethin'. Get goin'!

[Nishikawa exits to the left followed by the Captain.]

GOSUKE *[in a voice that gets gradually weaker]*: Hachizo, ya here? Hachizo?

HACHIZO: Well, calm down an' get some sleep. If ya sleep, ya'll feel better.

GOSUKE: Hachizo. Lemme tell ya why I don't wanna die. It's 'cause I don't want all a ya t'eat me.

HACHIZO: What the hell ya talkin' about! Dammit! Eat

ya? *We* eat ya? The hell with you! We ain't bears or wolves! Shut up with that kinda talk, hear!

GOSUKE: Ya won't eat me?

HACHIZO: What ya take us for? Some kinda bastards that eats human flesh?

GOSUKE: Hachizo, ya won't eat me after I'm dead then, will ya?

HACHIZO: I said I won't! I won't! How the hell can I when yer from the same village as me an' joined up on the same ship as me?

GOSUKE: If I wasn't from the same village an' didn't join the same ship, would ya eat me?

HACHIZO: Oh goddam ya! Cut it out! Cut that kinda stuff out! I hate listenin' to ya!
[Stands up and goes to the left.]
W-a-i-t, I'm goin' to the beach too. Now, Gosuke, take it easy. Awright?
[Exits. Gosuke stands up staggering. He walks a few steps forward and falls down. He raises himself with great difficulty and also exits to the left. The stage darkens.]
[Three days have passed before the stage lights up again. Gosuke is already dead, and the other three survivors are haggardly emaciated. Gosuke's corpse, placed at the innermost depth of the cave, cannot be viewed by the spectators. Only the Captain and Nishikawa are seen in the cave.]

NISHIKAWA *[crouching beside the fire]*: How I hate it!

CAPTAIN *[standing away from the fire]*: Ya hate it? No wonder ya feel that way. But look, Nishikawa, that makes ya a coward.

NISHIKAWA: I'm not a coward. But I don't eat human flesh.

CAPTAIN: It ain't that ya don't—ya can't!

NISHIKAWA: That's right. I can't.

CAPTAIN: Why not?

NISHIKAWA: Because it's not right.

ひ
か
り
ご
け

121

CAPTAIN: Why ain't it?

NISHIKAWA: —It's shameful to eat human flesh.

CAPTAIN: What's so shameful about it?

NISHIKAWA: Isn't it shameful to eat the flesh of your own comrade?

CAPTAIN: Ya gotta lot a real thinkin' to do. If ya don't like the idea, ya don't have to, and that's all there's to it. I'm not orderin' ya to. I'm only tellin' ya to because I don't want ya to die.

NISHIKAWA: I don't mind dying.

CAPTAIN: I know how ya feel. A nice young kid like you. When the ship was goin' under, you was the one that jumped into the sea with the rope. I know the kinda man y'are. Yer different than Gosuke or Hachizo. Ya work hard, sacrifice yerself, don't complain. Ya risk yer life outa loyalty. Ya do favors for yer shipmates. It don't surprise me ya don't feel like eatin' Gosuke.

NISHIKAWA: Then why do you keep insisting I do?

CAPTAIN: Ya don't care if ya die a dog's death after what we gone through?

[Nishikawa is silent.]

Don't ya want a glorious war death that'll get ya the Order of the Golden Kite? It looks like I gotta remind ya of a seaman's duty. I don't have to warn ya about rememberin' how important we are to the Army, do I?

NISHIKAWA: I couldn't forget that.

CAPTAIN: We're gonna die if we keep on like this. That's for sure. In this kinda mess, nothin's easier than just droppin' dead. If all we gotta do is die a hunger, we don't have to worry any more about duties, responsibilities. All we gotta be's scared and die a hunger without even tryin' to get on ship and servin' our country. Any lazy bastard or coward can do that.

[Hachizo enters trudging from the left. He joins the other two around the fire and warms his hands and legs in silence.]

CAPTAIN [seeing that Hachizo has no game]: Nishikawa, ya sure are scared a eatin', ain't ya?

NISHIKAWA: It's not that I'm scared. I don't feel I can.

CAPTAIN: Yer scared ya'll become a bad man once you ate. It's a sure thing ya wouldn't be no ordinary man once ya had some a it. That's what scares ya. Yer scared they might call ya a man that made it by eatin' human flesh. That scares ya so much ya think ya can save face just by not eatin' any.

HACHIZO: What ya talkin' about?

CAPTAIN: About eatin' Gosuke.

HACHIZO: Ah, there it is, like I thought. Didn't I tell ya we oughta float him right out t'sea?

NISHIKAWA: Hachizo, doesn't this kind of talk surprise you?

HACHIZO: Wish t'hell it did. It's a real puzzle t'me why I ain't surprised, but the fact is I ain't.

NISHIKAWA: Then you've been thinking about eating him too, Hachizo?

HACHIZO: I wouldn't go so far t'call it thinkin'. It just come into my head. T'begin with, it's bad that it come in. But once it's in, it won't go out. Let's float him away right now! I bet that's the only way outa this mess.

CAPTAIN: Hell ya will!

HACHIZO: We oughta have a funeral for Gosuke, huh?

CAPTAIN: We can give him a service anytime. What's importanter is how ya make up yer mind about this.

HACHIZO: Wonder if a funeral ever was where ya ate the corpse?

CAPTAIN: Once ya floated him away, it's over. Let's think hard about it before we go floatin' him away.

HACHIZO: All it takes is a little thought an' we'll be eatin' him. 'Cause all we got t'eat is Gosuke an' the only thing we been thinkin' a's food. So ya see there's nothin' for us to do but get rid a what starts us thinkin'.

ひ
か
り
ご
け

123

CAPTAIN: Hachizo, be honest and tell me ya don't wanna eat *that*.

HACHIZO: Well, I don't like the idea a eatin' Gosuke. But, honest, I do sometimes feel like eatin' *that* flesh.

NISHIKAWA: Captain, let's float him away right now!

CAPTAIN: Not on yer life! As Captain, I'm tellin' ya for yer own benefit. Understand? We ain't cannibals. We're Japanese in every way. It's natural not to feel like eatin' a shipmate. But just see how long we can keep up that natural human feelin'. Wait and see how long we can hold out.

HACHIZO: It's no good waitin'. Waitin's no good.

CAPTAIN: The truth is I ain't usin' rank as Captain in the kinda mess we're in. I ain't out just to have my own way for my own sake. I'm worried because the three of us has gotta pull through t'gether. See what I mean? How about waitin' two days? After that, what d'ya say we get up a funeral service for Gosuke?

HACHIZO: In two days nobody won't be able t'even move their ass.

CAPTAIN: Well, so we wait one day then. Till tomorrow night. Awright? Now we gotta bring in all the firewood we got by tearin' down the hut. It don't matter how it hurts us, we gotta least have a supply a firewood. Now let's go. Pretty soon we ain't gonna be able to move a inch. Now let's go.

[All exit sluggishly to the left. The stage gets dark.]

[Three days have passed before the stage is lit. Hachizo, already in extreme exhaustion, is lying on his back. Nishikawa is crouching beside him. The Captain is absent.]

HACHIZO *[in a very low voice]:* There ain't nothin' t'worry about. Honest, there ain't. I know yer a real good man. *[Nishikawa sobs.]* I know how ya feel. It's terrible t'a ate human flesh.

NISHIKAWA: I'm ashamed of myself.

HACHIZO: You bein' ashamed proves ya ain't a bad man.

NISHIKAWA: You didn't eat.

HACHIZO: I promised Gosuke before he died. I'da ate too if I didn't.

NISHIKAWA: Why did I eat?

HACHIZO: Outa loyalty. See, ya ate so's ya can work outa loyalty.

NISHIKAWA: No, it's not that. It's not that.

HACHIZO: Ya ain't t'blame. Ya'd be hungry if ya didn't. It's no crime when ya ate 'cause ya was hungry.

NISHIKAWA: The Captain told me, 'Wouldn't ya eat Gosuke if the Emperor ordered ya to?' I didn't say anything. Then the Captain said, 'Yer body ain't yers. It's the Emperor's. If the Emperor orders ya to defeat America, ya gotta. If the Emperor orders ya to kill Americans, ya gotta. Look, Nishikawa, if yer ordered to stay alive, ya gotta stay alive. If yer ordered to eat Gosuke to stay alive, ya gotta eat him.' That's what the Captain said.

HACHIZO: The Emperor wouldn't even know about us.

NISHIKAWA: No, he wouldn't. It's impossible he'd order us to eat human flesh.

HACHIZO: The Emperor's takin' it easy in the Imperial Palace. How can a man that ain't never been hungry once in his life be smart enough t' think about that? I'm sleepy now. I don't feel cold. I don't feel any pain. My hands and legs are stiff. Lemme get t'sleep.

NISHIKAWA: Please, stay up a little while longer. Like I said, that's the kind of thing the Captain told me. I'm beginning to be afraid of him.

HACHIZO: Ya gotta watch out for guys that's done things and come up with arguments. Ya gotta watch out for guys that tries to put their arguments across. I'm tired. Real tired. Lemme sleep.

ひかりごけ

125

NISHIKAWA: It's not out of loyalty I ate human flesh! I ate it for my own sake, that's all!

HACHIZO: I'll be dead soon. Lemme alone.

NISHIKAWA: There's still some flesh left for you. You'll get well if you just eat flesh!

HACHIZO: Ya'll have less left if I eat some.

NISHIKAWA: I don't intend to deprive you of your share!

HACHIZO: I know ya don't. But Captain does.

NISHIKAWA: The Captain said, 'Don't force nobody to eat what they don't wanna.'

HACHIZO: That sounds like him. He's been lookin' way ahead from the beginnin'. He keeps his head workin' way far ahead.

NISHIKAWA: Hachizo, is the Captain a bad man?

HACHIZO: Well, he's a quick one for good an' bad. He must be figurin' out now when I'll die. He must even be figurin' how many days after I'm dead my flesh'll last the two a ya.

NISHIKAWA: He's gone that far?

HACHIZO: Not only that. But he's figurin' after the time even when my flesh'll been ate up.

NISHIKAWA: . . . I'll be left alone with the Captain. Oh, I'm afraid!

HACHIZO: I hope, some way, ya stay alive till the end. You'd be honest an' tell everyone about us. There ain't no chance Captain'd do that. If ya die, nobody'll be tole how we died, what we thought a before dyin' . . . The fire burnin'? I can't see the light a the fire at all.

NISHIKAWA: It's burning all right.

HACHIZO: Really? My eyes must be gettin' weak then. Nishikawa? Just stand up for me. Stand up, please.

NISHIKAWA [*stands up mystified*]: See, I'm standing.

HACHIZO [*raises the upper half of his body with difficulty*]: Go further back. Further on into the back.

[*Nishikawa draws back little by little, facing Hachizo. By*

*and by, a ring of light, like the halo of the figure of Buddha,
is seen behind his neck, beaming a golden green light.]*

HACHIZO: Yeah, just like what I heard! Horrible!

NISHIKAWA: What? What's horrible?

HACHIZO: The ring a light behind yer neck.

NISHIKAWA *[turns his head right and left]:* I can't see it.

HACHIZO: Ya can't see it. I can, real good.

NISHIKAWA: You're seeing things.

HACHIZO: No. They say—an' it's handed down from
way back—that a man that's ate a man's flesh has a
ring of light come out from behind his neck. A golden
green light. A ring a pale, pale light comes out. Anyway, they say it looks like somethin' called 'luminous
moss.'

NISHIKAWA *[running back beside the blazing fire, the ring of
light fading out]:* No! That's impossible! You're seeing
things! Seeing things!

HACHIZO: I wish I was.

[Lies down again.]

NISHIKAWA: Do you still see it?

HACHIZO: No.

NISHIKAWA: Didn't I tell you? You just imagined it.

HACHIZO: No, I didn't. It ain't everybody can see that
ring a light just anywhere. Only certain people, when
they look in a certain direction, can see it just for a
second.

NISHIKAWA *[stricken with fear]:* Oh, I can't stand any of
this! I hate it!

HACHIZO: Ya don't have t'worry. I'm the only one can
see it. An' I'll be dead pretty soon.

NISHIKAWA: Hachizo, don't die. Don't die please! Stay
alive for me, I beg you!

*[The Captain enters from the left and silently looks inquiringly
at them.]*

NISHIKAWA: Captain! Hachizo's dying! He'll die too if
we don't do anything for him!

ひ
か
り
ご
け

127

CAPTAIN: We can't help it.

NISHIKAWA: Can't help it?

CAPTAIN: A man that don't like human flesh can't help dyin'.

NISHIKAWA: Doesn't it make you sad to have a shipmate die?

CAPTAIN: Even if I feel sad, a man that's dyin' can't be helped.

NISHIKAWA: Captain! You're waiting for Hachizo to die so you can eat him!

CAPTAIN: Even if I ain't waitin', Hachizo'll die. A man that's dyin'll die no matter what. A man that's alive gotta live.

NISHIKAWA: You don't care who dies just so you can eat his flesh!

CAPTAIN: I ain't no devil. Who wants to eat human meat? I'm just tellin' ya the truth. Just think. If Gosuke hadn't died for us, we'd both a died just about today. Get it? Remember, nobody asked him to die. He just died. So you and I ate him. Whatever way ya look at it, that's all there was to it. Before Hachizo dies, ya don't have to make a stink about whether to eat his flesh or not. I ain't sayin' it just for an excuse. When Hachizo dies, maybe I'll eat his flesh. Maybe ya will too, Nishikawa.

NISHIKAWA: I don't like it! I don't like it!

CAPTAIN: Me neither. Neither aus like it, but we'll end up eatin' his flesh.

NISHIKAWA [sobbing]: I don't like this! None of this!

[The stage gets dark.]

[Ten days have passed before the stage lights up. The flesh of Hachizo is already gone. It is becoming increasingly cold in the cave. The Captain's tenacious determination to remain alive is as firm as ever. Nishikawa has already lost something that sustains life.]

[The Captain, standing beside the fire, looks down at Nishi-kawa as he is sleeping. Nishikawa suddenly sits up, waking from a dream. He cries out in terror when he notices the Captain looking down at him. In the intense silence, Nishikawa stares at the Captain, who turns away.]

CAPTAIN: Ya ain't been sleepin' so good these days, have ya?

NISHIKAWA: But you have.

CAPTAIN: Oh, I sleep good enough. What's the use a worryin' about anythin' when yer in this kinda mess? I don't know why, but ya look scared. The least ya can do is get a good sleep.

NISHIKAWA: Even when I'm sleeping, I can't sleep.

CAPTAIN: That's just how ya look.

NISHIKAWA: And when I'm awake, I'm sort of sleeping.

CAPTAIN: Must be terrible to be like that.

NISHIKAWA: Yes, terrible. All the more terrible when I start thinking it's terrible.

CAPTAIN: The worse time must be just when ya open yer eyes after sleepin'.

NISHIKAWA: Yes. Isn't it the same with you?

CAPTAIN: Yeah, the same with me. My body and my head feel like hell. I ain't a bit different than ya.

NISHIKAWA: But your mind's not in pain, is it?

CAPTAIN: The hell it ain't. It's just that my mind, no matter how much pain's in it, ain't never troubled. I'm only tryin' to do what I thought a doin' in my mind. So I don't let myself get mixed up or worry myself sick. If ya end up worryin' yerself to death, it's better not to start worryin'.

NISHIKAWA: Whether I live or die, I can't help feeling horrified.

CAPTAIN: Must be awful feelin' that way.

NISHIKAWA: Isn't it to you?

CAPTAIN: All I want's gettin' rescued quick as possible. I ain't thinkin' a nothin' else.

ひ
か
り
ご
け

129

NISHIKAWA: We'll never be rescued. And even if we are, it won't help.

CAPTAIN: I know ya gotta grudge against me, Nishikawa. Ya do, since I made ya eat when ya didn't wanna. And not just a grudge against me. But yer scared a me, ain't ya? Yer scared I might kill ya and eat ya.

NISHIKAWA: Yes, I am.

CAPTAIN: That's why ya can't sleep, no matter how hard ya try.

NISHIKAWA: Yes, that's part of it. But it's not only because of that I can't sleep.

CAPTAIN: I won't kill ya. At least I won't do nothin' like that to ya.

NISHIKAWA: Why not kill me? Why not kill me and eat my flesh? Nobody'd know.

CAPTAIN: I ain't got no idea a killin' ya yet.

NISHIKAWA: If I die, there'd be nobody left to know what you did. That's how you expect things to turn out.

CAPTAIN: I don't have to kill ya. Ya'll die even if I don't do nothin'.

NISHIKAWA: So you're just holding out patiently, waiting for me to die?

CAPTAIN: It ain't that I'm waitin' for ya to die. I'm just waitin'. And while I'm waitin', it's in the cards ya'll die.

NISHIKAWA: That's much worse than killing.

CAPTAIN: That so?

NISHIKAWA: That's just what a really bad man would do.

CAPTAIN: That so?

[Lies down and stretches to his full length.]

Am I a bad man?

NISHIKAWA: Yes, you are.

CAPTAIN: I wonder if a bad man'd end up in this rotten

hole eatin' human crap and eatin' his own heart out about it. I bet a bad man'd be livin' in comfort, eatin' somethin' a little bit better.

NISHIKAWA: Captain, did you ever give a thought to Gosuke and Hachizo?

CAPTAIN: I can't help thinkin' about them. They're the men we ate.

NISHIKAWA: And don't you feel you're a monster?

CAPTAIN: Would ya be satisfied if I said I'm horrified at myself?

NISHIKAWA: I'm not asking for my sake. What are *you* feeling? That's what I want to know.

CAPTAIN: I'm bearin' up. I'm bearin' even what I can't bear. To bear up this much ain't easy.

NISHIKAWA: All you're doing is bearing up?

CAPTAIN: I ain't got no one else t'take care a me. I gotta bear anythin' and everythin' all by myself. When I say I'm bearin' up, I mean I'm bearin' up under every single thing. To bear up ain't so clear and easy as seein' a watermelon split clean in two.

NISHIKAWA: I can't bear up.

CAPTAIN: Once ya decide not to bear up, everythin's easy. To bear up's not a easy thing to do. Somebody else's bearin' up in yer shoes ain't *you* bearin' up. And there ain't no rule that says under what and how much ya gotta bear up. Ya don't know what the hell yer bearin' up for, and still ya keep bearin' up. That's bearin' up.

NISHIKAWA: How can we bear up when we don't know why we're bearing up?

CAPTAIN: It don't surprise me to hear ya say that. But tell me, can ya honestly tell yerself what's painful to ya? Can ya tell which is painful, ya bein' frozen, yer empty stomach, ya eatin' yer shipmates' flesh, there ain't bein' no hope a rescue? No, I bet ya can't. Ya never could. Everythin' mixed up with everythin' else

ひ
か
り
ご
け

131

must be painful to ya. So painful yer all messed up about just what the hell's painful. It's a same with me. I'm bearin' up so much I can't tell neither what I'm bearin' up under.

NISHIKAWA: You know damn well what you're bearing up under! You're bearing up while figuring how dead Gosuke would be followed by Hachizo and Hachizo by me! You're bearing up knowing damn well the order things are going to happen in!

CAPTAIN: Anybody can know that kinda order. Just because I know who's gonna die next ain't no reason I know what I'm bearin' up under. Well, well, bear up. Bear up and sleep. I'm tellin' ya that because ya can't bear up unless ya can sleep.

NISHIKAWA: I won't sleep.

[Takes up his self-made harpoon as if intending to murder. At the same time the ring of golden green light is again seen behind his neck.]

CAPTAIN *[raising the upper part of his body, perceiving Nishikawa's intention from his look]:* Ya gonna kill me? If that's what ya got in mind, I'll kill ya too. *[Behind the Captain's neck the ring of light also comes into being.]*

NISHIKAWA: I won't let you eat me!

CAPTAIN: Like it or not, ya'll be eaten if ya die. Ya can't help but be eaten.

NISHIKAWA: I'll make sure I won't be eaten by you even if I'm dead.

CAPTAIN: What ya gonna do? Escape?

NISHIKAWA: Yes!

CAPTAIN: Why do such a wasteful thing? If ya gotta drop dead, why not here? Put yerself in the place a the person that's gonna be left behind.

NISHIKAWA: I'll throw myself into the sea! I'll die where you can't lay your dirty hands on me!

CAPTAIN: Why do such a mean thing? I thought ya was a young kid that was more obedient, kinder.

Nishikawa: I'd rather have sharks eat me than you!
[Exits to the left, staggering with harpoon in hand.]
Captain: Nishikawa, wait! It's wrong to waste! Nishikawa! Wait, listen! What's the use a makin' me starve to death? *[Exits running after Nishikawa.]*

[From the time Nishikawa conceived the idea of murdering the Captain, sacred music has been heard faintly in the cave. The musical motif is taken from a song of the Ainu bear festival. Since the bear festival is a ceremony in which the celebrants send back the god that has brought them the gift of meat in the form of bears, their music contains a deep sense of gratitude so that one is made to forget the bloody act of bear killing. It is a warm and devout piece of music expressing joy over being blessed with meat as well as a wish that the god return safely to his home.]

[As Nishikawa exits, the sound of the music rises. As it is rising, the light of the fire diminishes. When the music reaches its greatest volume, the fire fades completely. At that moment, all the luminous moss in the cave beams forth its light, the profound and exquisite hue of golden green flooding the stage.]

[Soon the Captain, dragging the dead body of Nishikawa, enters from the left. The standing figure of the Captain and Nishikawa's corpse are seen only in black silhouette, their expressions and other details about them obscure. The Captain is naturally insensible to both the light from the luminous moss and the sound of the sacred music. The Captain lets go of the arm of the corpse and stands upright in the center of the cave. The music is gradually turning into a dance rhythm of quick tempo. Stricken with terror, the Captain crouches with his head in his hands. The light from the luminous moss fades out all at once. Only the ring of light behind the Captain's neck begins to beam.]

ひかりごけ

[The curtain falls while the sound of music continues.]

133

CHARACTERS
Captain
Various persons necessary to compose a typical court-
room, such as Judge, Prosecutor, Defense Counsel,
Spectators

SCENE
A court of law. A day in late spring six months after Act One.

PRODUCTION NOTES
*For the producer (that is, the reader) to carry out a good pro-
duction (reading) of this act, he should keep in mind the mode
of expression seen in the grotesque religious pictures of the
medieval European painters, Bosch and Breughel, or the painted
scrolls of medieval Japan. That is especially necessary in order
to create a turbulent but quiet atmosphere, as in a Passion
Play.*

*It is desirable for the Captain to be played by an actor other
than the one who performed the role in Act One. In Act Two the
Captain must be quite different in appearance, facial expression, and voice. The Captain of Act Two, his vicious look gone
forever, has a peaceful face like that of Christ. Most important, the Captain has an exact resemblance to the junior
high school principal who, as a guide, led the writer (accord-
ingly the reader) to Makkaushi Cave. If it is remembered that
it was no other than the principal who influenced the writer to
record the Pekin Promontory Incident from the remark that
"Fantastic characters really do exist!" the sudden transformation from the Captain to the principal will not be too
surprising. If Act Two, in which the hero has changed entirely, cannot be accepted as an extension of Act One, it may
be viewed as a separate unit, without relation to Act One.
The Captain of Act Two speaks a cultivated, standard Japa-*

nese, not the uncultivated language he used in Act One. This indicates that while the Captain of Act One could understand the meaning of "bearing up" only in an uncultivated way, the Captain of Act Two has an intelligent understanding of its meaning.

As the curtain rises, the stage is a law court flooded with dazzling rays of light. But the construction of the court reminds one somehow of the cave in Act One.

The banging of the gavel by the presiding Judge is heard as he attempts to stop the furious cries of agitated Spectators.

PROSECUTOR: I am opposed to the opinion advocated just now by the defense that the defendant was forced to eat human flesh because of circumstances beyond his control. Did not Gosuke and Hachizo die, for that matter, under the very same circumstances, without daring to partake of human flesh? And although Nishikawa, like the defendant, ate the flesh of a human being, he was overwhelmed with humiliation and was about to hurl himself into the sea when the defendant killed him. In contrast to the fact that these three victims each died after finally showing evidence, more or less, of human repentance or human suffering, we have the Captain as the lone survivor without revealing a shred of repentance, an iota of suffering. And if all this were not enough, even after his crime was revealed, the defendant has remained calm, and at the present moment is without the slightest trace of regret. This extraordinary, this arrogant attitude by the defendant in a court of law more than substantiates his criminal character.

The defense has cited as an example of justification a case during the Edo Period in which peasants, during

ひかりごけ

135

a time of famine, mutually exchanged their children in order to eat them. But that event took place more than two hundred years ago. And the incident is merely reported in an old newspaper. Not only that. We have no eyewitnesses to testify to its veracity. We must conclude that it has no possible relevance to this trial.

Finally, as for the defendant's patriotism, or some such thing, on which the defense has rested its case, that is absolute nonsense. It is, in fact, a flagrant outrage against the concept of patriotism. If, as the defense has advocated, cannibalism ought to be permitted for the purpose of survival at any cost in order to carry out one's patriotic duties, why did our loyal and brave soldiers, those hundreds and thousands of men who had exhausted their rations, why did they have to starve to death in distant battlefields overseas? *[Applause.]* Never must any comparison be permitted in the same breath between those loyal war dead who fought the hardest and starved to death for the sake of our country and this detestable, egocentric defendant! *[Applause.]*

Add to all of this the fact that the defendant is a Captain who is responsible for the important lives of his seamen. There are untold numbers of captains who went down with their sinking ships. This defendant devoured the flesh of his comrade-seamen, going so far as to kill the lone sailor that had stayed alive with him until the very end.

Driven to bay by our exacting inquiry, the defendant, at long last, confessed all the details of his crime, but as for his own feelings about his terrible actions, he has not as yet uttered a single word. As even the defense counsel has admitted, that is certainly beyond human comprehension. But it proves that the defend-

ant cannot bear to discuss his own unspeakable base-
ness or that, viciously sly by nature, he is merely remaining silent as a disguise to maneuver himself into
a favorable decision.

Obviously, the counsel for the defense has become too
emotionally involved in the question of the defendant's
own personal feelings. Instead, counsel for the defense
ought, first of all, to consider in his own heart how the
bereaved families of the victims feel, the families of
Gosuke, Hachizo, and Nishikawa. *[Applause.]* Is it not
a simpler, more obvious basis for judgment than any
other that one's sympathies ought to reach out to those
persons who had the flesh of their fathers, their sons,
and their husbands devoured? If we consider the grief
and tears and anger of these bereaved families, is there
any need to listen to what this despicable defendant
has to say about the feelings in his own depraved
heart?

COUNSEL: Your Honor, I submit the defendant be allowed to speak.

JUDGE: Thus far the defendant has been given a number
of opportunities to make a statement, but he has failed
to do so.

COUNSEL: Please grant him another chance.

PROSECUTOR: If the defendant can honestly confess his
innermost feelings, I too would like to devote my full
attention to what he has to say.

JUDGE: Well, the defendant may say whatever he has
in mind that he wishes to.

PROSECUTOR: No matter what the defendant may say,
his crime is already quite obvious, and the decision
unalterable. But since his crime is rarely to be met
with in this world, to know his psychological state as
it actually is may be of use for future reference. Counsel
for the defense has requested permission for the de-

ひ
か
り
ご
け

137

fendant to speak. Let him stand and answer our questions. *[The Captain stands up.]* I should like to know what you are feeling now. Aren't you feeling compunction, guilt—some such human feeling?

CAPTAIN *[in a sad voice]*: Must I answer?

PROSECUTOR: Yes! There's no need to impress anyone with that kind of preliminary!

CAPTAIN: I am bearing up.

PROSECUTOR: What are you bearing up under?

CAPTAIN: I am bearing up under a good many things.

PROSECUTOR: What do you mean by a good many things? Why not be frank and say quite specifically what you're bearing up under?

CAPTAIN: ... For example, I'm bearing up under this trial. *[The entire court is thrown into an uproar.]*

PROSECUTOR *[in an outburst of rage]*: You mean you're dissatisfied with being put on trial!

CAPTAIN: No, not that.

PROSECUTOR: If you aren't, how can you say you're "bearing up" under it?

CAPTAIN: I am not dissatisfied with this trial, but I am bearing up under it.

PROSECUTOR: Can't you put that a little more simply? The way you've phrased it, it strikes me as if you're merely quibbling to confuse us.

CAPTAIN: I am not dissatisfied with this trial, but it seems to me the trial has nothing to do with me.

PROSECUTOR: Nothing to do with you? Don't you remember the grave crime you've committed? You know you have, don't you?

CAPTAIN: Yes, I do.

PROSECUTOR: Hmm. You admit your crime. Then why keep up this fuss about bearing up or not? It's quite natural for you to be put on trial, isn't it?

CAPTAIN: But ... I mean, I have nothing to say except that I am bearing up.

PROSECUTOR: Perhaps you think you can't make yourself understood. That's just what I've been saying accounts for your extraordinary arrogance. The very way you keep saying you're "bearing up" under this trial and the like simply proves you are flattering yourself that you're superior to us, doesn't it?

CAPTAIN: No, I have no such intention. I never once thought I was superior to others.

PROSECUTOR: Then you might be a little more frank and honest.

CAPTAIN: It's impossible for me to be more frank and honest than I have been. . . It is simply that I have been bearing up under a good many things. . .

PROSECUTOR: You certainly seem to be strong in bearing up! But let's put it another way. You're impudent, aren't you? It's been my experience that not only you, but all scoundrels, as everyone knows, are each and everyone quite strong in bearing up.

CAPTAIN: I don't remember ever trying to lie my way out of anything wrong. I simply said I am bearing up because I am.

PROSECUTOR: What good has your bearing up done you? Your bearing up, which you seem quite skillful at, has it enabled you to do one single good thing?

CAPTAIN: No, it hasn't.

PROSECUTOR: And still you are going to insist on your bearing up?

CAPTAIN: I bore up *at that time* while thinking I had to. And this time as well. I am merely bearing up with the same feeling I had *at that time*.

PROSECUTOR: I've never come across a scoundrel as glib as you! Is that all you want to say? I doubt if you've left anything unsaid though, having spoken at such great length!

CAPTAIN: May I ask you a question?

PROSECUTOR: What question? Go ahead, ask.

ひ
か
り
ご
け

CAPTAIN: Mr. Prosecutor, what kind of food did you eat from December of last year to January of this year?

[The court is disturbed by angry and spontaneous cries.]

PROSECUTOR *[grinning reluctantly]:* You want to know that? I ate a variety of things, but, I can assure you, at least I didn't eat the flesh of a human being.

CAPTAIN: I see. I have another question I want to ask you. Mr. Prosecutor, have you ever had your own flesh eaten?

PROSECUTOR *[with excessive irony]:* Fortunately not. None of *my* colleagues are as vicious as you!

CAPTAIN *[more and more sadly]:* Those are the two things I wanted to know about you. Now I understand quite well.

PROSECUTOR: You do? You say *you* understand, but I don't. Enlighten me.

CAPTAIN: Do I have to answer?

PROSECUTOR: Answer at once!

CAPTAIN: But it's useless if I answer.

PROSECUTOR: Even if it is, answer!

CAPTAIN: I cannot feel I have been judged if the Prosecutor judges me.

JUDGE: Your statement cannot be allowed if you are not more careful in your choice of words.

PROSECUTOR: Your Honor, I don't mind. Let him speak up, please. So, you don't want me to judge you? Why not me? Whom do you want then? Who could possibly be someone you wouldn't complain about?

CAPTAIN: Gosuke or Hachizo or Nishikawa would do. Otherwise. . .

PROSECUTOR: The men you mention happen to be dead. Not only that, but aren't they the men you ate from their hands down to their feet? You'd like to have the dead judge you? Obviously, by making that request, you're attempting to escape being tried.

CAPTAIN: I have no intention of escaping from anything.

I am only saying that I don't feel myself judged if you judge me.

COUNSEL: You better tell him why.

CAPTAIN: The reason is that the Prosecutor has not eaten any human flesh or had his own flesh eaten.

PROSECUTOR: Well, now I understand. Now I understand quite well what you want to say. You're implying that no one can perform the duties of a prosecutor unless he himself is as base as the criminal.

CAPTAIN [*quietly, as if in soliloquy*]: No, I am not. I mean nothing of the kind.

PROSECUTOR: But you do. You certainly fit the proverb, "Capture a thief and you'll find arrogance." You're trying to blame society or the nation for your crime. I tell you we are judging you on behalf of the nation and society! There's no doubt you don't take for granted our right to judge you. You want to deny us righteousness.

CAPTAIN: No, I don't. All I'm saying is that I wish a person who has eaten the flesh of a human being or has had his own flesh eaten to judge me.

PROSECUTOR: Your Honor, have you heard his words? They clearly indicate the kind of character he has. The defendant is hopelessly irredeemable, a truly evil man.

JUDGE: Doesn't the defendant feel he has committed a wrong? Don't you feel any willingness to submit to sentence?

CAPTAIN: I would feel it was quite in the nature of things even if I were sentenced to death.

JUDGE: If that is so, why oppose the Prosecutor?

CAPTAIN: I don't believe I have ever opposed him. I have spoken only because I was forced to. I would not have said a single thing if I had not been told to speak up.

PROSECUTOR: That's a lie! You're lying! You're using

ひ
か
り
ご
け

141

whatever means you can to overthrow the authority of the court!

CAPTAIN: No, I have no such intention. I am simply bearing up.

PROSECUTOR: Now I have you! You probably want to say that no one in this court has the right to judge you. You want to escape punishment for your crime by insisting we're the same kind of human beings you are. No, I won't allow you to do that! Now let me remind you of the crime you committed. Did you begin with the finger or ear when you ate Hachizo? Did you peel Nishikawa's skin from his belly or his back? When you tore off the nails, tell me what sounds did they make? When you chewed at the flesh, how did it feel in your mouth?

CAPTAIN: . . . Mr. Prosecutor, perhaps you ought not to permit your imagination to run wild on things you haven't experienced.

PROSECUTOR: You are entirely incapable of humiliation, of humiliation, I tell you!

CAPTAIN: I am only bearing up.

PROSECUTOR: What you've done is bound to blemish the dignity of all the Japanese people! Bound to degrade the dignity of the nation! Have you no sorrow for the Emperor that you've done such things!

CAPTAIN: . . . It doesn't seem to me he is so different from me.

PROSECUTOR: What! What are you saying! Not different from you!

CAPTAIN: Is he not also merely bearing up?

[The court is thrown into an uproar. The Judge furiously bangs with his gavel.]

JUDGE: I forbid the defendant to speak!

[The air-raid siren zooms throughout the court. Panic-stricken, the crowd runs back and forth in the courtroom. Before one realizes it, the sound of the siren is turned into that of a snow-

storm. As the courtroom becomes darker, the stage comes more and more to resemble the rock-cave.

COUNSEL *[whispering into the Captain's ear]:* It's beyond my power to defend you any further.

CAPTAIN: Don't worry about that. Didn't we know from the very start this would happen?

COUNSEL: If I were the Prosecutor, I'd have felt like getting angry with you too.

CAPTAIN: Certainly you would. No wonder the Prosecutor became angry. Though I had no wish to anger him. It's just that I was told to answer no matter what. . .

COUNSEL: But you deserve pity. If you hadn't eaten, you'd have starved to death. And once you did, you committed a crime. You were fated for misfortune.

CAPTAIN: I don't think I'm particularly unfortunate.

COUNSEL: You aren't?

CAPTAIN: No, I'm not.

COUNSEL: If that's true, there can't be anything I can do for you, can there?

CAPTAIN: No. No one can do anything for me. That was how it was in the cave. It's that way in court too.

COUNSEL: You're too much for me. You're just about the most easily resigned person I've ever met.

CAPTAIN: No, I'm just the reverse. Oh, I'd forgotten. I have only one thing I would like you to do. But it's next to impossible for you to do it.

COUNSEL: What's that?

CAPTAIN: To have me eaten. To have all my flesh eaten just as I ate Gosuke's, Hachizo's, and Nishikawa's. Can you do that? No, you can't. It's out of the question, isn't it? Well, don't worry about it. Nobody wants to do something like that. I only wish that man at least *[points to Prosecutor]* could eat me.

PROSECUTOR: Why do you single me out? Do you mean to say I'm some special kind of man?

ひ
か
り
ご
け

143

CAPTAIN: No, I don't. Only I. . .

PROSECUTOR: Or do you mean to say I'm a man that's eaten human flesh?

CAPTAIN: No, I don't. You're not like a man that eats human flesh. You're a prosecutor. You're honorable and decent. All the people here are honorable and decent. I'm the only one that has eaten. I'm the only one. No other person has.

[As the Captain is speaking, the stage becomes darker and darker, and the sound of the snowstorm rises increasingly. The music played at the end of Act One begins to be heard very faintly.]

CAPTAIN: All of you can clearly distinguish between yourselves and me. I have a ring of light behind my neck. Look at me closely. You can see it if you look closely. That's part of the evidence against me.

[A ring of light glows behind the Prosecutor's neck. Successive rings of light are seen glowing behind the Judge, the Defense Counsel, and the Spectators. No one is aware of his own ring of light behind his neck or of any other person's. The people in the crowd, with rings of light behind every neck, are still running helter-skelter.]

PROSECUTOR: Are you still talking nonsense? What's that about a ring of light? You say I can see it? Well, I can't. Can the Defense Counsel see anything?

COUNSEL: I can't see anything either.

CAPTAIN: I'm the only one with a ring of light. It's my mark.

PROSECUTOR: If you had such a mark, there'd be no need for a trial.

CAPTAIN: No, there wouldn't. Please look at me closely.

PROSECUTOR: Your Honor, can you see anything?

JUDGE: How can I see anything?

CAPTAIN: It can't be that you are unable to see it.

JUDGE: You say you can see it?

CAPTAIN: I can't see it. But you, other people, ought to

be able to. Look closely. Come nearer please and look closely.

COUNSEL: Why are you so certain you're the only one who can't see it?

CAPTAIN: Those who wear it can't see it. Those who have done *that* can't see it.

COUNSEL: But even I can't see it!

CAPTAIN: You can't? No, that's impossible.

COUNSEL: Neither the Prosecutor nor the Judge can see it!

CAPTAIN: What? If that's true, what a terrible thing is happening! You've got to come closer and take a good long look at me. It's impossible for you not to see it. You can't do this half-jokingly. You've got to keep staring, more intensely, until you see it.

[The Judge, the Prosecutor, the Defense Counsel, and some of the Spectators form a ring of figures around the Captain. They look like the ring of spectators surrounding Christ as He was being taken to Golgotha for execution. The Captain is hidden behind the hedge of figures.]

CAPTAIN: Please look at me. Please, look at me closely.

[With the number of people surrounding the Captain several times increased, rings of light gather tightly in great numbers.]

[While the Captain is crying, "All of you, please look at me," the curtain falls quietly.]

ひ
か
り
ご
け

145